Bet You'll Marry Me

By Darlene Panzera

Bet You'll Marry Me

Bet You'll Marry Me

DARLENE PANZERA

AVONIMPULSE
An Imprint of HarperCollinsPublishers

*For my children, Samantha, Robert, and Jason,
and my husband, Joe, who have supported
my dreams every step of the way.*

Acknowledgments

THANK YOU TO Debbie Macomber and everyone at Avon Books/HarperCollins for your enthusiastic support. I am deeply grateful for all you have done for me.

Bet You'll Marry Me

Chapter One

THE HIGH-SPIRITED NEWSPAPER boy spread the Saturday edition of the *Cascade Herald* on the bakery counter and pointed to the bold block-letter headline MARRY HER AND WIN.

"Look Jenny, you made front page!"

Jennifer Leigh O'Brien couldn't move. Couldn't breathe. Couldn't tear her gaze from the scandalous stomach-turning print. *Marry her and win?*

"I sold a hundred papers the first hour," the twelve-year-old continued. "By dinnertime I'll have enough money to buy the bike Karen's family is selling on page ten."

Jenny glanced at the nearly empty canvas news bag slung over Josh Hanson's shoulder, then at the compassionate face of her older friend, Sarah, who owned the bakery.

"They're placing bets on who I will marry?" Jenny's thoughts darted back to the one time she'd come close to marriage. *Disaster!* "And they announced it in the newspaper?"

Sarah set down a tray of fresh-baked cinnamon rolls. "You know how this town loves a good bet."

"Why can't they bet on the size of Reverend Thornberry's prize tomatoes, or how much of Levi MacGowan's home brew will be consumed at the Fourth of July fair?"

Sarah sighed. "Because people are always more fascinated by the actions of other people."

"The café is filled with people waving fistfuls of money," Josh added. "There's even men we've never seen before."

Men who would try to flirt with her!

Jenny drew in a sharp breath and searched the store for a weapon. The last thing she needed, or wanted, was a man's attention, or any attention for that matter. Why couldn't they leave her alone?

She moved toward the broom propped against the bread cart. Grasping the long yellow handle like a baseball bat, she gave it a test swing. "Mind if I borrow this?"

Sarah's eyes widened and the lines on her forehead doubled as she hurried around the counter of donuts, biscuits, and scones. "Jenny, you can't be thinking of—"

She nodded. "I'm going over there."

"What on earth for?"

"I have to stop them."

"With a broom?" Josh laughed. "Cool."

"But you've avoided the café on every trip into town for six years," Sarah said, twisting the hem of her apron. "Why go over there now?"

Jenny shot her a look over her shoulder as she walked toward the door. "To let those idiots know they can't mess with other people's lives."

AFTER WAITING TWENTY minutes to get in, Nick found a seat on the far side of the Bets and Burgers Café.

Everyone was talking about her. Three men in front of the gas station took turns boasting who Jennifer O'Brien would find more attractive. At the bank five people withdrew funds to bet on who she would marry. Then, on the street in front of the bakery, Nick paid a newspaper boy for a copy of the *Cascade Herald*, with the headline MARRY HER AND WIN.

This certainly threw a wrench into his plans. He hadn't expected the young woman to be a celebrity. How could he possibly hope to win her heart when every other man in town was trying to do the same?

He spread the newspaper on the café table and took another look at the photo beneath the headline.

Rob Murray had been dead wrong. Miss O'Brien was anything *but* a fat, hairy inbreed with missing teeth. In fact, she had beautiful teeth, a big bright smile. Nice features.

He thought about what he had to do and a weight lifted off his chest. He might actually enjoy this.

A short, balding, red-faced man stood behind the café drink counter writing on a giant chalkboard. One of the men called out his name, identifying him as the owner, Pete.

"Twenty on Ted Andrews and fifteen on David Wilson," Pete announced. "Anyone else?"

"Those two don't have a chance," said a man at the table to Nick's right. "I bet my money on Charlie. He has a way with the ladies."

A blond-haired waitress with bright cherry-red lipstick targeted him from across the room and made her way over with her order pad and tray.

"Can I get you anything?" she asked, wetting her lips with her tongue. "Coffee? Steak sandwich? My phone number?"

"Beer," Nick said, brushing her hand off his shoulder, "and a date with Miss O'Brien."

The waitress's expression soured, and a small dent formed between her manicured brows. "Everyone wants to waste their money on her, when they can have me."

"And they can have you for free, right, Irene?" added a man with sandy hair who dropped into the chair beside him. "You can bring me a beer, too. Whatever you got on tap."

Irene's full lips pushed into a perfect pout and she left to get their order.

The sandy-haired man laughed and introduced himself as Wayne Freeman. Taking a pack of cigarettes from the rolled-up sleeve of his T-shirt, Wayne nodded toward the frenzied betting scene at the back of the building.

"Jenny won't marry any of them."

"Why not?"

"Just look at them," Wayne said, gesturing toward the men. "They're all the same. Like a herd of sheep. Any man who wants to win Jenny will have to do something to get her attention. Something to set himself apart from all the rest."

"Like what?" Nick asked, hoping the man had some ideas.

Wayne waited until his cigarette was lit, then leaned back in his chair, making it creak like a rusty car door. "I've been a hired hand on her ranch for the last two years and I still wouldn't know."

"You work for her?"

Wayne nodded. "The O'Briens took me in after I lost everything I owned to my ex. I work the fields, look after the cows with the other hands, and they give me food and a pillow for my head. Jenny has a big heart, but she hasn't been interested in romance since she was jilted."

"Everyone's been jilted at one time or another. Maybe she hasn't met the right guy."

"Maybe," Wayne agreed, "but whoever wants to marry her will have to take drastic measures to win her over."

Nick thought about all the beautiful, dazzling young women he had dated in the past. They would do anything for jewelry, a press photo, and a little one-on-one attention. Handling women was like handling a business deal. They might pretend to play hard to get at first, but in the end they all negotiated.

His tension eased and he crossed his arms over his chest. Just because this girl rode horses and lived out in the country didn't mean she was any different.

A woman was a woman after all.

JENNY STOMPED ACROSS the main street of the rustic two-block town wishing she'd brought her shotgun. Or perhaps a bulldozer to knock the sleazy café and all its slimy bet-wagering occupants back into the infernal snake hole they came from. But even that wouldn't be good enough. Maybe the only thing to wipe the Bets and Burgers Café off the eastern slopes of the Washington Cascades this afternoon would be an old-fashioned keg of dynamite.

She narrowed her gaze on the handful of men socializing on the wooden-plank porch in front of the café entrance.

"Marry me," David Wilson called out as she approached, "and I'll split the money with you fifty-fifty."

As if she would ever marry him, a man three years younger whose intelligence was on a par with his hound dog! Stepping onto the porch, she gave him a wide berth.

"I'll recite poetry every night," Kevin Forester promised.

Some might appreciate it, but she wasn't the poetry kind of girl. Just straight-up honesty would suit her better than flowery words rolled off a sugarcoated tongue.

Ducking under his arm, she avoided his intended blockade, circled the colorful Native-American totem whose tribe once inhabited the area, and ran into Charlie.

"Marry me, Jenny," Charlie Pickett sang in a rich tenor, "and I'll dedicate my first recorded song to you."

Music wasn't exactly her thing either. She had nothing against it, but Charlie wasn't interested in pleasing her, he only sang for himself. Who knew? Maybe someday he'd be famous. Then he'd leave town like so many others and never miss the ranching community he left behind.

"Out of my way, Charlie," she said, giving him a hard push aside. "Let me through."

"Marry me and I'll help ye find the gold."

Gold? What gold? Jenny turned toward the familiar wheezing voice and old Levi MacGowan winked at her.

Jenny raised her brows. "Are you proposing to me, too, Levi?"

"You bet I am," he announced with a thump of his cane. "I figure I got as good a chance as the rest of them."

"Didn't you just hear your grandson David propose to me?"

"Yeah, but I'm better-looking than he is."

David Wilson smirked. "Grandpa, you are too old for her."

"And you're too young," Levi said with a frown. "You'd best leave her be."

The cane slipped from Levi's hand and Jenny latched on to his arm so he wouldn't fall.

"See what a good wife you'd make?" Levi crowed.

"A good wife is more than a support post," Jenny countered, and retrieved the hand-carved wooden stick for him.

"Ouch!" Levi chuckled. "Feisty, today, are we?"

"Sorry, Levi. You know I love you," she said, and her tone softened, "but these other men—"

She clenched the fiberglass handle of the broomstick she carried with a grip that could break a mountain beaver's neck. Only a high-stakes bet could bring this many people out at one o'clock on a hot Saturday afternoon. Heart hammering, she drew a deep breath and walked through the café door.

"Thirty dollars on Kevin," someone inside shouted.

"Fifty says Charlie can get Jenny to marry," yelled another.

The run-down café hadn't changed since she'd last stepped foot in it six summers ago. Pete Johnson was still taking bets. His daughter, Irene, still sashayed her hips as she waited on the men and women sitting at the dozens of rough-hewn cedar tables. The same raucous laughter interrupted the music from the overhead stereo. And the same bitter taste gathered at the back of her throat. Yep, nothing had changed, except she wasn't as young this time, wasn't as weak, wasn't as naïve.

"One hundred dollars on Ted Andrews," Pete bellowed as he faced the chalkboard. "Only a brave man can slap down that kind of cash." Then the café owner turned to search the crowd for more bets.

And spotted her.

"Pete, don't you dare duck behind that counter," she said, and pinned him with a sharp look.

The short, bald-headed man responsible for the wagers straightened from his abrupt half crouch. "Come to see who's in on the bet?"

"No." She marched toward the back of the room and raised the broomstick she'd borrowed from Sarah's Bakery. "I've come to teach you a lesson."

"Jenny!" Irene shrieked, running to grab hold of her arm. "Don't do it!"

She shook off the trashy, promiscuous blond and her mind reeled with horrific memories of the bets they'd placed six years earlier. Bets that left her standing at the altar alone. Bets that led to Irene's presence in her former fiancé's bed. Bets that kept her from wanting to enter the café ever since.

Until *today*.

Using every ounce of her strength, Jenny swung the broomstick across the top of the counter, shattering the dozens of drink glasses into a million glimmering pieces.

The accompanying high-pitched crash was so loud it was a wonder the mirrors on either side of the chalkboard didn't decide to jump off the walls and shatter with them. Beer, soda, and glass sprayed across the floor. Women gasped. And the men closest to the counter jumped back, swearing and cussing like the untrustworthy, self-serving pigs she knew them to be. Then a bewildered hush ricocheted across the café as every pair of eyes focused their questioning gaze on her.

"Here you are, Pete," she said, and handed him the broom. "You'll need this to sweep up the mess."

Pete scowled. "You're going to have to pay for this."

She pointed to the chalkboard advertising her name. "The money from your bets should cover the damage."

Pete's face reddened. "That's not fair."

"Fair?" She scanned the scores of unapologetic faces,

both male and female, that surrounded her. "You call making bets on my life *fair?*

"I should call the sheriff," Pete warned.

"Go ahead," she retorted. "And I'll have you shut down for illegal gambling. Or maybe I'll convince him to put me in solitary confinement. That would put an end to your bets."

"Heck, Jenny, we all know your financial situation," Pete said with a shrug. "Now that the bank has given you a deadline, you'll have to marry to save Windy Meadows. And we're just placin' a few friendly wagers on who we think the lucky man is going to be."

"I don't need to marry anyone."

Pete continued as if he hadn't heard her, "So far we have four main contenders: Charlie Pickett, Kevin Forester, David Wilson, and Ted Andrews."

"Don't forget about me," old Levi cackled from the other side of the room.

"And Levi," Pete amended, and the crowd broke into laughter.

Jenny pursed her lips. "I can just take in another investor."

"The last one took off with half a year's profit," yelled Charlie from the doorway.

Okay, so she'd lost out big on that one. She'd made a mistake. But there were other ways to save the ranch.

"I can sell off equipment at the upcoming auction."

"Your father sold everything he could before he died," Kevin said. "You don't have anything left."

"I have the steers" She lifted her chin. "And the horses.

I came into town today to hand out flyers advertising the guided pack trips I plan to lead up Wild Bear Ridge."

Pete's brow quirked. "You think pack trips will save Windy Meadows from foreclosure?"

"Four generations of my family are buried on that land," Jenny said, emphasizing each word. "Do you think I'm going to let anyone take *them* away from me?"

"You might not have a choice," David said, coming through the door behind Kevin and Charlie. "Unless you find the gold."

Gold? Jenny frowned. David's grandpa Levi had also mentioned gold. "What gold?"

"The gold your great-great-grandfather discovered on the property," Pete explained.

"I don't know what you're talking about."

Pete pulled a printed page from behind the counter. "It's right here in this entry of his journal."

Jenny stared at the piece of paper. It was a photocopy of a page from her great-great-grandfather's journal, all right. One of the old dusty volumes she'd loaned to the town historian the week before.

Pete pointed to the writing. "Ole Shamus O'Brien says here that the other guys found gold along the river bordering your property, but *he* found a gold mine. The entry is dated October twelfth, eighteen eighty. A week later, he passed away from pneumonia, and we're all guessing the gold is still there."

"If there was a gold mine hidden at Windy Meadows, I would know about it. I've covered every inch of that land and I—"

Right before the barn fire took her father's life, he'd dug five holes on the far side of the property, toward the eastern border. He'd said he wanted to plant trees. Trees he never bought. Did her father know what was in her great-great-grandfather's journals? If he believed a gold mine was on the property, wouldn't he tell her?

"Is *that* why everyone wants to marry me?" Jenny demanded. "To get the gold?"

What had she been expecting, that one of the men actually held feelings for her? Secretly loved her? Of course they didn't love her. They barely knew her.

She'd kept her distance from most boys since Ted Andrews stuffed a lizard down her jacket back in grade school. From that day on, she'd realized the male gender couldn't be trusted. And the one man she'd thought had been different had only reinforced her opinion when he slept with Irene Johnson on their wedding day. Nope, the only men she could count on were her daddy, God rest his soul, and her uncle Harry and cousin Patrick. *Family.*

She knew better than to let her emotions take hold of her, but she couldn't help it. If there was one thing she couldn't stand, it was deception.

"You're despicable. All of you. Anyone with any decency at all would loan me the money I need to save my land. But no. Here you are placing *bets*. And why? Because you believe there's a stupid gold mine on my property." Her whole body shook with rage. Fire burned through every pore of her skin. "If you want something to believe, believe this—there isn't any man here who can get me to marry!"

A tall, dark-haired man she had never seen before emerged from the crowd and slammed a green check down on the table beside her.

"Ten thousand dollars says you'll change your mind."

Jenny stared up at him. He topped her by at least six inches. Then she glanced down at the numbers scrawled on the check. A wave of openmouthed gasps rounded the room, followed by a single resounding, drawn-out whistle.

"What?" she demanded. Was this a joke?

"Ten thousand dollars says that within five weeks you'll marry *me*." Pushing back the brim of his black Stetson, he looked into her eyes with an expression of pure confidence.

"You—you must be out of your mind."

"I've never been more serious."

"So if I don't marry you, and I win," she said, flustered by the way his silver-gray eyes studied her, "I get your ten thousand."

"Yes."

"And if you win . . . ?"

"I get you."

Her body lurched with an involuntary start, and she struggled to regain her composure. "What's your name?"

"Chandler," he said, never taking his eyes off her. "Nick Chandler."

"You're on."

She accepted his challenge with outward calm, but her stomach twisted into a lasso of knots as Pete laid out the rules.

"The bet ends Saturday, July thirteenth, at one o'clock in the afternoon. Winner takes home the check. Agreed?"

Jenny hesitated. "Thirteen is an unlucky number."

"Not for me," said the man by her side.

Jenny locked eyes with the dark-haired stranger. "Even if you were the most charming man on the face of the earth, there's no way I'd ever agree to marry anyone in just five weeks."

"Sometimes," Chandler said, arching his brow, "five weeks can seem like a lifetime."

Jenny knew she wouldn't be able to keep up her bravado much longer. She needed to run away. *Fast.*

She turned to leave, but a hand on her shoulder spun her around, and she found herself pressed up against her newly acquired opponent instead.

Her first thought was to reach down and draw out her boot knife, but before she could react, his warm lips brushed across her own.

What perverse, mind-warping insanity led her to think she could stop the bets? Here it was, six years since the last time her name was on the chalkboard, and she hadn't learned her lesson. She was still humiliating herself in front of everyone in this confounded café!

"My money's on Chandler." Old Levi MacGowan's voice rang out as more gasps and guffaws erupted around them.

Jenny pushed away from the brash newcomer and retaliated with a slap. A hard slap. She caught her breath as the left side of his tanned face turned a glorious dark pink.

Chandler didn't flinch. The hit must have stung like

the spines of a devil's club plant, yet it didn't stop him from smiling at her or looking at her with a mischievous twinkle in his eyes.

With all the courage she could muster, she held her head high and walked out the door.

Nick stared after her, transfixed by her fleeing image. She wore no makeup. She didn't need to. With her eyes flashing like a dark blue thunderstorm and her auburn hair whipping around the room every time she turned her head, she was a natural beauty. But it was the look of concern flickering across her face after she smacked his cheek that caught his attention. And the uncertainty in her eyes as she walked away.

The ranch hand he'd met earlier that day slapped his back and placed a congratulatory beer in his hands. "Bolder than a bugling bull elk in rut," said Wayne Freeman, shaking his head. "A little too bold, if you ask me."

Nick grinned. "Care to bet on that?"

"Not if I want to keep my job." The sandy-haired man nodded toward the door. "You just butted horns with my boss."

AFTER CHECKING INTO the Pine Hotel, the only one in the flea-sized Northwest town, Nick went to his room and called N.L.C. Industries. He glanced at the clock while listening to his cell phone ring, calculating the time difference between the East and West Coasts. It was after four thirty in New York but his vice president, Rob Murray, would still be there, even on a Saturday.

"Did you meet with the O'Brien woman?" asked Rob, his tone anxious.

Nick rubbed the left side of his face. "Yeah, we just had our first encounter."

"And?"

"She may take a little more time than I anticipated. Instead of a weekend, I might have to stay out here in Washington a few weeks."

"Weeks? What if, after all that time, you still can't sweet-talk the land away from her?"

"I might have to do more than sweet-talk. When I got here I learned I'm not the only one interested in getting my hands on her property. Some of the locals are willing to marry her for it."

"Marriage?" Rob repeated. "You can't be serious."

"I don't see any other way. If I don't marry her, someone else will. Then we'll never get the land."

Nick recalled the honest emotion racing across the redheaded beauty's face. Jenny O'Brien was *not* like any of the other fake, flirting, foraging females he'd dealt with most of his life. As far as he could tell, there wasn't anything phony about her, something he found irresistibly refreshing. It also made him feel like a first-rate jerk for having to deceive her.

"Why you?" asked Rob. "Isn't there someone else who can seduce the woman?"

"No one I can trust to get the job done right."

"Of course," Rob said, his voice lit with amusement. "So who's going to run the company while you're gone?"

"You are. Think you can handle it?"

"Yes, sir!"

"I'll do what I can from here on my laptop, but I might not be able to check in with you every day. And, Rob?"

"Yes?"

"Don't put your feet up on my desk. This is only temporary."

Rob laughed on the other end of the line. "Got it."

Next, Nick punched in the number to his younger sister, Billie. Now that he'd gained Miss O'Brien's attention, he needed a way to get close to her. Wayne Freeman had unknowingly given him a pretty good idea how to do it, and he was going to need Billie's help.

Chapter Two

JENNY LEANED FORWARD in the saddle as Starfire prepared to jump. Her fingers firm and steady on the reins, she pressed her knees to the horse's sides. Starfire's muscles bunched beneath her and a moment later, they sailed into the air, not as high as they used to, but still clearing the gate by half a foot.

No doubt about it. The best remedy for stress was a good ride. Starfire landed and the wash of emotion that swept over her was similar to the relief she felt when an airplane touched down on the runway. Relief, not because she was afraid of flying but because she was home. On Windy Meadows property. Where everything was familiar. Everything was safe.

Jenny brought the thoroughbred's pace down to a slow trot, and headed straight for the stable.

The long wooden structure housed eighteen stalls, a

wash area to bathe the horses, and a wonderful oversized tack room. Besides the multitude of hooks and cabinets full of horse equipment, the tack room was filled with her favorite photos, trinkets, and best-loved treasures.

She could sit in the tack room for hours, leaning against a comfy bale of hay, reading a book or dreaming of her next adventurous trail ride up to Harp Lake. Countless times when she was little, she'd sneak out of her bedroom late at night and sleep here, in this special place, instead of her own bed.

As she slid out of the saddle, the sweet smell of horse and hay soothed her senses like her own personal brand of aromatherapy. Neighs from the other horses blended together to sing her favorite song. Their friendly faces greeted her with warmth and understanding.

Why couldn't the townspeople understand her resolve to keep the ranch? Hadn't they ever loved anything so much it would kill them—rip out their heart and soul—to let it go?

And why did they think marriage was the only solution to her financial dilemma? Maybe they expected her to be like the other young women who either kicked off their cowgirl boots on the way to the city or married the first guy who asked them to dance.

She wouldn't sell Windy Meadows. And she wouldn't hitch herself to a man she didn't love, no matter how good a dance partner.

The audacity of that conceited, dark-haired man to bet he could convince her to marry him. Nick Chandler had no idea who she was or what she liked or didn't like.

He didn't know her past, or her present hardship, or her dreams for the future.

And what kind of man kissed a complete stranger? He appeared to be in his early thirties and was dressed like the other ranchers, wearing a T-shirt, jeans, and a black Stetson hat. But instead of dirt, sweat, and leather, he smelled like a new shirt straight from a Fifth Avenue store. And when he touched her . . . his hands were smooth. Too smooth to have done much ranch work. Could he be a city slicker out on vacation?

Whoever he was, he'd foolishly bet her ten thousand dollars, and the temptation to acquire some easy money had been too hard for her to resist. All she had to do was avoid the man for the rest of June and the first two weeks of July and the ten thousand would be hers. *Half her bank debt.*

Combined with the money she received from the pack trips, she'd be debt free a full month before her end-of-summer deadline. Wouldn't *that* surprise everyone?

Staying beyond Chandler's reach for five weeks would be easy enough. He couldn't pursue her if he never came into contact with her. She'd just stay on the ranch. There was a ton of work that needed to be done, and she couldn't afford to take time off to go into town anyway, even for church.

Jenny sent up a little prayer hoping God would forgive her and make the days fly by faster than usual. Then after she won the bet, Nick Chandler would go back to wherever he came from.

Where *did* he come from?

She'd love nothing better than to stay outside with the horses all day, but duty called, and a stack of bills waited for her in her father's office.

Jenny trudged up the back steps to the house and picked up the first envelope on the dark mahogany desk. Another buyout proposal from N.L.C. Industries. A quick toss into the trash can took care of that one. The next set of bills took more time.

Competition from other countries had caused the value of beef to drop and the change in climate patterns had also taken its toll. Yes, profits were down—way, way down—and she wasn't certain how to cut costs. She'd ridden horses most of her life and dabbled in medicine. She didn't have a degree in business. Why, if her father were still alive . . .

She swallowed hard. If her father *were* still alive, he would be the one struggling to operate Microsoft Excel and balance the ranch's profit-and-loss statement.

Two hours later, Jenny shut off the computer and frowned at the sudden rise of voices below. Someone was talking to her uncle Harry and it didn't sound like any of the ranch hands.

She leaned her head through the open second-story window and spotted a blue Ford pickup parked outside—a rental from the looks of it, because no one she knew could afford a truck with so much shine. The chrome finish could dazzle a blind man.

A thread of panic laced her steps as she hurried downstairs. Had N.L.C. sent another corporate front man to make her an offer in person? After waving a shotgun in the last guy's face, she hadn't expected them to return.

Ready to ambush the intrusive company representative with a verbal assault, she nearly ran straight into the young woman with short caramel-colored hair coming through the back door of her kitchen.

"Who are you?" Jenny asked.

"Billie."

She stared at the Yankee baseball cap and black Budweiser T-shirt the woman with the small boyish frame was wearing.

And the blue luggage in her hand.

"What are you doing here?"

"No idea." Billie scowled and pushed past her. "But right now I'm taking my suitcase to my room."

Did Uncle Harry invite this tomboy character here? And if he did, why didn't she know about it? Shaking her head, Jenny left the kitchen and went outside.

She took three steps across the porch—and locked gazes with the same silver-gray eyes she'd spent most of her sleep-tossed night trying to forget. She froze, her breath caught in her chest.

No. It couldn't be.

The dark-haired man with the black Stetson tipped the edge of his hat in greeting. Her uncle Harry turned and motioned for her to join them.

"Jenny, I'd like you to meet—"

"Chandler."

Saying his name was like chewing sour huckleberries on an empty stomach. The unpleasantness went way down.

"I've just hired him to be our new ranch manager," Harry said, sticking the shovel he was holding into the ground.

"What?" She began to feel claustrophobic, like the whole world was closing in on her. Which is an odd feeling when you live on a hundred acres. "But Harry, *you* are the ranch manager."

"And you need me to accompany you on the pack trips. We need someone to look after the ranch for us, Jenny, and Nick's our man."

"Th-that man," she stammered, "bet ten thousand dollars he can get me to marry him."

Harry turned and leaned on the handle of the shovel. "Is that right?"

"Yes, sir," Nick Chandler informed him, clearly not intimidated by Harry's hard, scrutinizing look.

Jenny stared back and forth between them, breathless, and waited for her uncle to throw him off the ranch. Any minute now . . . *any* second . . .

The corners of Harry's pale blue eyes crinkled, and he let out a hearty chuckle.

"Good luck, son," he said, extending his hand.

Chandler shook it. "Thank you, sir."

Jenny gasped, unable to believe her ears, and Chandler shot her a mischievous grin.

"So who is the girl in the house?" she asked, and her voice not only cracked but rose an octave.

"My sister Billie." Chandler's voice was deep and smooth.

"Billie's going to cook for us," Harry explained.

"Harry," she said, and stepped off the porch, "can we talk about this?"

Chandler's gaze followed her. His expression dared her to try to change Harry's mind. She returned his look with one of her own. One that said *Watch me* as she pulled her uncle away.

Harry Fisher, her mother's brother, had come to live at Windy Meadows after his wife's funeral, when Jenny was ten. Her father, who believed Harry possessed an impeccable ability to judge character, put him in charge of hiring the other ranch hands and never once questioned his choice of men. And neither had she. Until *now*.

She couldn't allow Harry to keep this man on the ranch, but she had to be careful not to step on his authority, either. Harry took great pride in his decisions and she didn't want to hurt his feelings.

"I didn't know you were planning to hire anyone," she said, keeping her voice soft so Chandler couldn't hear.

"I wasn't," Harry admitted. "Nick just showed up. He asked if we needed an extra hand and the more I talked to him, the more I thought about it."

"But ranch manager?" Jenny asked. "Do you really think he's qualified for that position?"

Harry put a big, burly arm around her shoulders.

"He's more than qualified. He and his sister grew up on their grandfather's ranch in Upstate New York, and Nick used to ride rodeo."

This isn't working, Jenny thought, and bit her lower lip. She needed to change tactics.

"Harry, you know what a financial mess we're in. How can we afford to hire someone right now?"

"I'm going to give him my salary."

"But—"

He put up a hand to silence her protests. "What do I need money for? I have a bed to sleep in at night, food in my belly, breath in my lungs."

"We could use your salary to save the ranch."

Harry shook his head. "Nick can help us save the ranch. He has a degree in business."

"A degree doesn't mean he's good."

"My gut instinct tells me he is."

"What about his sister?" she demanded.

"Nick says Billie is epileptic and he's responsible for her. He promises she can cook and help out in the stable for free if we let her stay here with him."

"She's another mouth to feed."

"Ah, but not a big one."

Jenny peeked over Harry's shoulder as Nick Chandler and his tiny sister took more luggage out of the truck. Their contrast in size was so great, she wouldn't have believed they were related except for the identical silver-gray eyes.

Harry followed her gaze. "I gave them the two extra bedrooms upstairs."

"You invited them to sleep in the house?"

"Well, I couldn't have Billie sleep in the bunkhouse with the men. It wouldn't be right."

"Okay," Jenny said, and threw up her hands. "Why can't *Chandler* sleep in the bunkhouse?"

"He says he needs to stay close to his sister at night."
Harry shrugged. "Says she has nightmares."

"Nightmares," Jenny repeated, and pursed her lips.
She didn't believe a word of it.

Billie appeared to be about her own age. Twenty-eight?
But the young woman's attire, scowl, and belligerent tone
during their encounter on the stairs reminded her of a
juvenile delinquent. Tough. With attitude.

"I can't imagine that girl being afraid of *anything*,"
Jenny said, shaking her head.

"Why does it matter where they sleep?"

"I don't want that man anywhere near me, that's why."

"Afraid he might win the bet?" Harry's blue eyes
twinkled.

"Of course not."

"Then there's no problem."

"Yes, there is," Jenny said. "I'm sorry Harry, but I
insist he goes."

"And *I* insist he stays."

"But—" Jenny stared at her uncle as he planted his
boots, drew himself up, and appeared ten feet taller. She
swallowed hard, sure she felt her nerves tremble.

"Jenny," Harry said, using a tone she hadn't heard
since she was a child. "I need him."

Need him? She hesitated. Her uncle didn't need anybody, but he was keeping something from her. And she
was too afraid to ask why.

"Give him a week," Harry said, his voice firm, "then
you can fire him if you want to."

"One week," she agreed.

Her uncle smiled and turned back into the man she'd always known and loved. "Thank you, Jenny. It will all work out, you'll see."

Uncle Harry headed toward the corrals and Jenny wiped her sweaty hands down the sides of her jeans.

One week. Then she'd get some answers.

BILLIE STRUGGLED TO haul her other suitcase up the narrow flight of wooden stairs in the big cedar house.

"I thought a ranch was supposed to only have one floor," she complained.

Nick didn't let her sour mood bother him. In fact, his plan had worked so well, he was springing up the steps.

"This is an old farmhouse," he said, and took the suitcase from his sister's hands. "Did you see how big the kitchen is?"

"Of course, since that's where I'm supposed to prepare everyone's meals. How could you do this to me? You know I can't cook."

"Then it's time you learned."

"I won't do it," she said, jutting out her jaw.

Sometimes Billie could irritate him to no end.

"How else could I convince them to let you come on to the ranch with me?"

"I don't know. I thought that crazy story about me being epileptic was pretty good," she said, her hands on her hips. "Nick, we don't belong here. This is never going to work, and now you've wasted ten thousand dollars on a stupid bet—"

"The bet drew Jenny O'Brien's attention."

"It sure did," Billie drawled. "I think she hates you."

"Billie," he pleaded, and glanced down the stairs to make sure no one was listening, "the only reason I'm doing this is for *you*. You're the one with the hundred-thousand-dollar gambling debt. Do you have any idea what Victor Lucarelli will do to you if you don't get the money to pay him back?"

"I'd rather not think about it." Billie's face blanched. "I made a mistake."

"Two mistakes," he corrected, following her to her bedroom. "First you cheated the casino owner—didn't even *think* the security camera might catch you in the act, and then you lost all his money to someone else."

"It was supposed to be a private game of poker and I was mad at Lucarelli for being so haughty." His sister set her suitcase down and walked around in a circle. "Nice room."

"It's not the Hilton."

"Cedar plank walls. Creaky floorboards. Remember when we were little and I was convinced there was a ghost on Grandpa's ranch? I stayed up all night waiting for it to appear so I could spray it with Silly String."

Nick grinned. "Then you would be so tired you wouldn't wake up in the morning."

Billie looked down at her feet and then up at him. "Nick, do you think Lucarelli and his men will kill me?"

"They'd have to kill *me* first," he said fiercely.

"I'm sorry." Billie sounded more sincere than he'd ever heard her. "I'm so sorry."

"I know." He drew in a deep breath. "If I can win the bet and get Jenny to marry me, the O'Brien land will be half mine. I'll have the missing piece of acreage I need to sell my land tracts to Davenport. Not only will we have the money to pay off your debt, but we'll have money to buy Jenny another ranch to live on."

Billie shrugged. "So what do you want me to do?"

"Become Jenny's friend," he said, nudging his sister with his shoulder. "From what I've learned from the people in town, she could use a good friend. Find her weak spots. Give me an edge so I can get close to her."

"You never needed my help with a woman before," Billie teased. "Do you really think you can get her to marry you?"

Nick grinned. "Go study some cookbooks."

Chapter Three

After a restless night's sleep Jenny awoke early, threw
on a pair of jeans and an old T-shirt, and tied her long
hair up in a ponytail.

Had she overreacted to her uncle's decision to hire
Chandler? The work on the ranch kept everyone busy
from sunup to sundown. Surely the chances of the man
having any spare time to bother her would be slim.

She was wrong. Nick Chandler fell into step beside her
as she made her way down to the stable.

"How about you and I go for a ride this evening? You
could show me the layout of the land on horseback."

"That's Harry's job," she said, and then cast him an
appraising look. "Besides, you won't be up to it."

"What's that supposed to mean?"

"It means those smooth hands of yours, which are no
doubt accustomed to delicate office work, will be covered

in blisters by nightfall. You won't be able to hold on to the reins long enough for an evening ride."

Chandler winced, as if she'd punched him in the gut.

"If I *am* able to hold on to the reins," he said, shooting her a sideways glance, "will you ride with me?"

"No."

"Why not?"

"I don't want to."

Josh Hanson, her young newspaper-delivering neighbor, came from behind and ran between them. "The only one who can get a date with Jenny is *me*. She gives me riding lessons every Monday."

Nick tipped his hat toward the boy. "Great idea."

"Forget it, Chandler," Jenny warned and turned toward Josh. "You can get Echo ready and meet me in the arena."

Josh ran ahead, and when Jenny reached the stable she found Harry arguing with Frank Delaney.

"Managing a ranch is hard work," Harry shouted. "I need someone who will take on a challenge, not hide behind it. I need someone assertive."

"Well, you certainly are assertive," Jenny muttered, and glanced at the dark-haired man beside her.

"I heard that," said Chandler, giving her a wink.

"I'll show you assertive," said Frank. His upper lip curled as Chandler approached. "We'll just see who the better man is."

Frank snatched a saddle off the rack and went out the back door in a huff.

"He's going to be a problem," Jenny predicted.

"Nah. He'll cool down in a couple of days." Harry

took a brown leather bridle from one of the hooks along the wall. "What do you think? Should we have Nick ride Satan?"

She hesitated. Satan had been her father's horse. Although he desperately needed to be exercised, the temperamental black quarter horse had been difficult to control since her father's death six months ago. She doubted Nick Chandler could stay on him ten minutes, let alone a full day in the fields.

"No, I don't think he could handle him."

"I can handle any horse you give me," Chandler insisted.

How could he be so sure he could handle an animal he knew nothing about? In her opinion, it was high time Nick Chandler got knocked down a notch. Riding Satan would probably knock his bolstered ego down *several* notches. Would it be enough to make him quit?

"Yes," Jenny said, amusement bubbling up within her. "Let's put him on Satan."

JENNY LED THE horses from their stalls to the outside paddocks, fed them their morning flakes of alfalfa, then met Josh for his riding lesson.

The twelve-year-old, who lived two mailboxes down the road from her, had already tacked up the small chocolate colored Arabian with a western saddle and bridle.

"Bring her up to a jog," Jenny instructed, and entered the white-fenced circular arena. "That's good. Loosen the reins, and sit straight, no slouching."

"When are you going to let me help drive the cows back and forth between the pastures?"

"When you're ready," Jenny said with a smile. "First you need to practice your sharp turns."

"Do you think I'm fast enough to enter the Pine Tree Dash?"

"That's a tough race," Jenny told him. "Not only do you have to be fast, but you have to maintain control. Do you think you could keep control of the horse at a gallop?"

"If I were in open fields instead of an arena, I bet I could gallop faster than an airplane can fly." The boy gave Echo a small kick and sped the horse's gait from a jog to an easy lope.

"Good job, Josh. Be careful with the reins. You don't want to jerk the horse's mouth."

"That's what my dad tells my mother," Josh said, circling around. "He says she forces him to complain."

"What does your mom say?"

"That he tortures her on purpose to make her quit the marriage."

Jenny thought of Nick and wondered if Satan had tortured him enough to quit the ranch.

"I'm sorry to hear your parents are having problems. It must be hard on you and your sisters."

"Yeah. Everyone in town is betting on who you will marry and they're all betting if my parents will divorce."

Jenny grimaced. "They place bets on any idea that pops into their head."

Josh cut across the arena, first in one direction, and

then another. "Have you ever met a *person* you can't get out of your head?"

"What? Yes. Yes, I have." Jenny had to suppress a laugh. Every moment since she'd met Nick Chandler she couldn't stop thinking of ways to get rid of him.

"I mean," Josh said, as he came around again, "when you see them you feel like you can't breathe—like you have asthma or something."

"Like when a bully backs you into a corner at school?"

"Not a bully," Josh said, riding past her. "But someone you kind of like. My friend Zach has an asthma inhaler he uses at school. I asked him if it helped when he was around girls, but he said he didn't think so."

"Girls?" Jenny smiled. "Do you like one girl in particular?"

"Maybe." Josh slowed the horse to a walk and came over to her. "Jenny, what do you think of dating a younger man?"

A younger man? She didn't think of dating at all. Well, maybe once in a while—but only in a fantasy-world, remote kind of way.

She frowned. "Did David Wilson put you up to this?"

"No," Josh sputtered, color rising into his cheeks. "I'm asking for myself. I just wanted to know how you felt about it."

"I don't think age matters too much as long as there's love."

"Great!" Josh averted his eyes, and blushed even more. "I mean—good to know."

Jenny gasped. Did Josh have a crush on her? She'd

thought the reason he'd been hanging out at her ranch so much was to avoid the turmoil at home, but maybe she was wrong. Maybe he hadn't been joking when he'd bragged to Nick earlier. Did Josh think *he* had a chance to win the bet?

How cute! What an adorable, sweet, little boy!

"Josh," she said slowly, "is this why you want to take riding lessons—to impress a certain girl?"

The twelve-year-old nodded, while keeping his head bowed. Then he looked up and his expression changed to one of complete anguish.

"Karen Kimball is fourteen, two whole years older than me, and she enters all kinds of competitions. Her family has the bicycles for sale and I really want one. It would be great to ride a bike when I deliver newspapers, but if I go over there I'll have to talk to her and nothing comes out of my mouth when I try to talk to her. I shouldn't even like her. But she catches bullfrogs with her bare hands, and tips the canoe over in the lake on purpose, and is always teasing me. But I like the way she teases me. It's not the way my parents tease each other. My parents always fight and scream and lock each other out of the house. No wonder you don't want to marry. I don't want to marry either. But I can't stop thinking about this girl."

"Karen Kimball." Jenny swallowed hard. Of course Josh hadn't meant *her*. She was too old for him. Why would he have a crush on her? She was only interested in her horses. She never did anything with anyone else. She always did things . . . alone.

"Don't tell anyone I told you," Josh pleaded. "I don't usually talk about this stuff. Zach thinks I'm crazy. But I thought you'd understand because of the way you look at Nick."

Jenny bristled. "How do I look at Nick?"

"Like you secretly like him."

"I do not!" she said in a rush. "He's arrogant and manipulative, and he's not even staying on the ranch for very long. He'll be gone within a week."

"Don't worry," Josh said, moving back across the arena. "I'll keep your secret, if you keep mine."

NICK EASED FORWARD in the saddle to adjust his tired seat. His thighs ached, his back ached, his hands were raw, and to top it off, he *did* have a few blisters. Jenny would feel smug about that.

What was he doing on this pitiful run-down ranch? He was a businessman with contracts to sign. He didn't belong here and the other ranch hands made darn sure he knew it.

Every available moment, they'd drive the cattle in different directions. At lunch they filled his saddlebag with manure, and in the afternoon one of them drove a tractor through the fence he'd fixed.

"It's one thing to try to woo some girl," said Wayne Freeman, all the friendliness from the café absent from his face, "and another to think you can worm yourself onto this ranch and tell us what to do. Frank and I were here long before you strolled into town."

Even worse than the ranch hands' disloyalty was the

fact Jenny planned to lead some of the other bet-wagering cowboys on an overnight pack trip into the mountains.

Harry said Jenny had expected families and 4-H groups to sign up for her pack trips. When the men from the café signed up instead, she'd almost backed out. Except each pack trip could bring in two thousand dollars and she needed the money. Nick shook his head, despair seeping into every muscle of his overexerted body.

Harry was going with her. Still, the other men would have a better shot at winning the bet—unless he gained her affection first. That incredible feat was going to require every ounce of charm he could muster, and at the moment, he wasn't sure he was up to it.

As he drove the last of the cattle into the corral for the night, Nick forced Satan to a halt and the black gelding snorted with annoyance. If it wasn't the ranch hands testing him, it was the horse. At least the horse finally knew who was boss.

Pushing his hat off his forehead, Nick wiped the sweat from his brow with the back of his hand . . . and saw Jenny sitting on the top rail of the corral fence.

She waved to him, an eager expression upon her face, almost as if she'd been anticipating his arrival. He must be mistaken. He turned and looked behind him but no one else was around.

He slid out of the saddle as she approached, and fed Satan another of the special apple and molasses horse treats he'd used as bribery to keep him under control.

"Come to check on me?" he asked, managing a grin as he closed the corral gate and secured the lock.

"Heck no. I came to check on the horse." Jenny took the reins from his hands and ran her fingers down one of the animal's front legs. But contrary to her claim, her eyes were on him and not Satan.

"Care to go on that ride with me?" he asked, knowing full well she'd refuse.

"Yes, I would."

"You *would*?" He swallowed hard. When he'd dismounted, his legs had nearly buckled beneath him. Climbing back up into the saddle would be like climbing N.L.C. Industries' New York office tower—without any superhero strength.

Jenny fed Satan a carrot and then turned to look at him, her bright blue eyes sparkling with mischief. What was she up to? Then a brilliant smile escaped her lips and he found it didn't matter. It was the first real smile he'd seen on her, other than the one she wore in the newspaper photo. And in person, it was even more enticing.

His heart rate doubled, and his resolve renewed. This was the chance he'd been waiting for, the chance to spend time alone with her, and for that he would hoist himself back into that saddle or die trying.

A few minutes later, Jenny led two fresh horses from the stable and handed him the reins of a feisty chestnut that had its ears pinned back and its teeth fully exposed.

"Don't you have any horses with a calm disposition?" he asked, unable to keep the irritation out of his voice.

"Of course." Another smile parted her lips. "I just thought an expert wrangler, such as yourself, would prefer to ride a horse with a little more spirit."

"Spirit?" He pointed to the animal's threatening stance. "Is that what you call this?"

Jenny laughed and he suddenly had a pretty good idea why she'd agreed to ride with him. *Torture.*

Rounding the upper loop trail, Jenny frowned as Nick Chandler coaxed the wild chestnut into an easy lope. How did he *do* it? She had never been able to control that horse, but she wasn't going to let *him* know that.

Jenny sensed Chandler gaining speed behind her.

"Race you!" she called, and pushed Starfire forward with a slight squeeze of her legs.

She rode parallel to the river and couldn't help but scan the embankment. Parts of it were steep where the water had washed away the dirt under a mass of overhanging tree roots. Other areas held large boulders tightly locked within the river walls. But she didn't see any caves or indentations filled with mineral deposits. If her great-great-grandfather had found a gold mine, where could it be?

Ahead, the logjam jump came into view. Leaning forward, Jenny adjusted her weight in the English saddle and prepared to soar into the air. Except once again, Starfire didn't get the height he normally achieved. They made it over but his back hoof scraped the top of the barrier.

Seconds later, a startled whinny pierced the air, and when Jenny looked back, Chandler was lying on the ground. He wasn't fool enough to try to go over the jump in a western saddle was he? Western saddles weren't meant for jumping. She didn't even know if the horse he rode knew how to jump. Starfire was the only one of her horses that had been trained in both English and western disciplines.

Slowing Starfire, she slid off his back and ran across the meadow to Nick's side. He wasn't moving.

Panic coursed through her limbs, making her tremble. She shouldn't have tried to race him, shouldn't have brought him out here. She knew he had been in no condition to ride after his work in the saddle all day. What if he'd suffered a concussion? Or broken his neck?

He lay face up with his eyes closed, and didn't appear to be breathing. She had trouble breathing herself as she pressed her fingers to his throat and checked for a pulse.

Thank God, he was still alive. She recalled the new medical guidelines she'd seen on the Internet and gave him thirty hard, fast chest presses to keep his blood circulating. Then she tilted his chin up and opened his mouth with her finger. Nothing seemed to be blocking the airway. She pinched his nose closed. Took a deep breath. Lowered her mouth to his to perform CPR.

She was about to blow air into his lungs when the world rolled over, placing Chandler on top, with a very dark, calculating look in his eyes.

Jenny thrust Chandler off to the side, pulled out her boot knife, and sprang to her feet. "You *faked* that fall!"

"And *you*," he said, pointing to the crazed horse prancing about the field, "deliberately put me on that beast to torture me. What are you going to do now? Stab me?"

She followed his gaze to the tip of her boot knife, its sharp point glistening orange from the setting sun. What was she thinking?

"I—I'm sorry," she said, and trembled as she sheathed the knife beneath the hem of her jeans. "You seem to bring out the worst in me."

"Oh, well, you know what they say," Chandler said, pulling himself off the ground.

"What?" she demanded. Had the townspeople been talking about her again? "What do they say?"

"There's a fine line between love and hate."

"In your case," she said, hardening her expression, "that fine line is a brick wall."

She walked away from him and headed toward a giant apple tree fifty feet away.

"Where are you going?" Nick asked, following her.

"The cemetery."

There was no gate. Jenny swept her gaze over the names carved into the headstones, and knelt beside the newest, the one without any moss or age spots. The grave of her father, George O'Brien.

"There's so many of them."

Chandler's voice was filled with awe. What did he expect from a family cemetery?

Jenny tossed away a few of the apples that had fallen from the tree above and landed on the grass beside the graves. Then she pointed to the oldest stone, which was also the smallest. "My great-great-grandfather Shamus O'Brien left Ireland in eighteen seventy-six with his wife and young son. He traveled across America to Washington State, built the ranch, and then died in eighteen eighty, during the area's second short gold boom."

"The man with the gold," Nick commented.

Jenny pointed to another grave farther to the right. "This is my grandfather, Sean O'Brien. When I was little, he sat me on his knee and told me the reason they buried family on the property was to ensure the land would never be sold—never slip into the hands of developers. He said he'd rest easy knowing the land would always belong to one of his descendants."

"That's why you won't sell," Nick said, and ran a hand through his hair.

"No, I won't sell," Jenny said, and turned to face him straight on. "So if you think you can come here, and marry me, and sell the land out from under me, you can forget it."

"What if I just want to ranch?" Nick asked. "What if I'm just so taken with your beauty that I'd like to stay here forever . . . with you?"

Jenny smirked and rolled her eyes. "I know you must have an ulterior motive for betting me the ten thousand. I also know how valuable the land could be, if I didn't owe so much debt. I've had offers from several large companies to buy the land."

"Which ones?" Nick asked, crossing his arms over his chest.

"N.L.C. Industries is the most bothersome." Jenny scowled. "I'm beginning to think there isn't anything that company won't do to get their hands on my land."

Nick chuckled. "I've heard they are tenacious."

"Tenacious isn't even the word." She blew out a huff of disgust. "The company is in league with the devil."

"That bad?" Nick raised his brows.

"Oh, yes," she assured him. "Rumor has it the company needs to sell the properties it purchased here in Pine. Except *my* land sits smack in the middle of theirs, and no prospective buyer wants a useless donut-hole tract. They want my land, Windy Meadows, included in the deal."

"Sounds like N.L.C. Industries is screwed," Nick said, nodding his head.

"Serves them right for purchasing land around me in the first place, thinking they could run me out and build some smog-ridden industrial plant," Jenny retorted. Her blood boiled and her heart pounded just talking about it. "Do you know last month N.L.C. had the gall to offer to have the graves of my family relocated?"

"That's awful," Nick agreed.

"Where would they move them?" Jenny demanded, rising to her feet. "My family doesn't belong in some public cemetery on the other side of town. This is their home, the place they lived and loved and watched their children grow. Can you imagine seeing the caskets of your loved ones being pulled from the ground, unearthed from—" Unable to continue, Jenny shuddered.

"I imagine it would be haunting," Nick said, his face drawn, as if he, too, was affected by the image.

"Ghastly," Jenny amended. "No, I don't have any sympathy for N.L.C. Industries. As far as I'm concerned, they've dug their own grave."

Chapter Four

NICK HAD NEVER been happier to drop into a bed. For dinner, Billie made a green-noodle casserole which he overheard the ranch hands say tasted even worse than it looked. Deciding to forego trying the dish himself, he'd climbed the stairs, and laid down with an empty stomach.

It seemed he'd only had a few minutes of sleep when an urgent pounding on his bedroom door roused him back to full consciousness. Was it morning already? He glanced out the window toward the rising sun and heard Jenny's voice, followed by footsteps running down the hall.

Nick tossed his sheets aside, walked across the room and opened the door a crack to see what was going on.

"The steers are scattered," Jenny explained. She hopped up and down in the sunlit hallway and pulled on one of her boots. "Harry says they've wandered on to N.L.C. Industries property. We need every available person to help find them—including your sister—who seems to sleep very well for a person who's supposed to have nightmares."

Nick dressed as quickly as his tired limbs would let him and knocked on Billie's bedroom door. No answer. Turning the knob, he let himself in. Billie was sound asleep. He tried to shake her awake, with no results. When Billie slept, she slept hard.

Retrieving a cup of water from the bathroom he splashed his sister's face. It worked. Billie sprang up off her pillow and out of bed within seconds.

"I've told you before I hate it when you do that!" Billie yelled. "Now my bed is all wet. It better be dry before tonight or I'll make you switch rooms with me."

"Get dressed," Nick told her. "The cattle are trampling all over N.L.C. Industries' precious property and Jenny needs to round them up before the company owner finds out."

Billie laughed. "A little late for that."

Nick made his way down to the corral. The gate was wide open, and not one steer could be seen inside. Harry barked instructions to Frank Delaney. Wayne Freeman mounted a horse Jenny brought out to him and took off toward the river.

"Who closed the gate last night?" Harry demanded.

"I did," Nick said, joining them.

Harry frowned. "Was it shut tight?"

"Yes."

"Not tight enough," Frank drawled.

Not only had he closed the gate, but after he and

Jenny returned from their ride, he'd chained it as well. The chain was now missing, which meant someone was trying to pin the blame on him.

He narrowed his gaze on Frank. Now wasn't the time or place for a face-off, and pointing fingers wasn't going to win him any friends. If anything, it would only alienate him further from the ranch hands. Deciding to keep quiet about the chain, he moved off to saddle Satan so he could round up the herd.

"BE GENTLE," JENNY WARNED. She handed the reins of a small pinto over to Billie. "My horses respond to voice commands and don't need extra kicks or excessive tugs on the bit."

"I promise I won't hurt him," Billie said, hoisting herself into the saddle.

"Are you sure you can ride?"

For a moment Billie looked like she was about to lash into her with an assortment of colorful language, but then the young woman took a deep breath and replied, "Yes, I can ride."

Billie told the truth. The young woman kept up with an easy gait, and handled the pinto quite well when they circled a small group of steer at the far end of the field.

Even more of a surprise was the way Billie's brother systematically drove the scattered herd into one large group. Jenny paused for a moment to watch.

If Nick Chandler was still saddle-sore from the previous day, he didn't let it show. Racing first in one direction, and then another, he completely dominated the field.

Where did he learn to negotiate hairpin turns like that? On his grandfather's Upstate New York ranch? Or the rodeo circuit? She'd thought the dark-haired cowboy had lied when he'd recited his resume, but there was no doubt the man had past ranching and riding experience. Did he just change the direction of the entire herd? Jenny straightened in her saddle. Rarely had she seen such expert precision, even in skilled professionals.

"Got to admit, he's good," Wayne said, riding beside her.

"Harry only hires the best." She tore her gaze away from the dark-haired cowboy in the nice-fitting doeskin chaps and tried to change the subject. "Have you contacted Michelle?"

"She won't take my calls," Wayne said, his voice tight. "Geez, it's been almost two years since I've seen my little girls. I doubt they even remember me. If I had the money, I'd get a lawyer to enforce my visitation rights."

"I wish I could help you," she told him, "but I have creditors calling me day and night."

Billie rode toward them with a stray calf.

"You're too tiny for ranch work," Wayne called out to her.

Billie scrunched her nose and made a face at him. "And you're too sweet. I thought you had to have a better vocabulary than that to be a real hard-nose cowboy."

Jenny laughed. "Wayne Freeman, meet Billie Chandler."

Beads of sweat ran down the side of his face as Nick brought in the last of the herd.

"If you hadn't left the gate open, this never would have happened," Frank said, loud enough for everyone within a mile to hear.

Was he right in suspecting Frank? Or could Jenny have been the one to remove the chain off the gate? Was she trying to frame him? Or worse—did she have Frank do it? Did she think if she got him fired she'd win the bet?

After he unsaddled Satan, he went back up to his room and found she'd left him a gift.

Centered on the small round table next to his bed was a big white bottle of hand cream.

Jenny brushed Starfire and was humming him a soft, rhythmic song when Wayne leaned over the half door of the stall.

"Harry will fire him after what happened today, don't you think?"

"It wasn't Chandler's fault," Jenny said, moving around the back of the horse to brush his tail.

"But he left the gate open," Wayne insisted.

"No, he didn't. I was there. I saw him use the new lock and chain Harry bought at the hardware store."

"No one said anything about a chain," Wayne said. He scratched the blond stubble along the side of his jaw. "Jenny, you're not defending him because you're interested in him, are you?"

"Certainly not." She put the brush away and picked up a comb to untangle the snarls in the horse's mane.

"Do you think," he said, his voice strained, "you could ever take an interest in me?"

Jenny stopped what she was doing to stare at him.

Wayne had never tried to flirt with her in any way. His wife had been her best friend. Then two years ago, Michelle had taken their two little girls to Florida, never speaking to Wayne or her old friends again. Not even Michelle's mother, Sarah, who owned the bakery, could contact her.

The divorce had been hard on Wayne. It was even harder when Michelle cut a deal to sell their ranch to N.L.C. Industries. Left with nothing, Wayne had come to Windy Meadows and Harry had hired him on as a ranch hand in exchange for food and a bed in the bunkhouse next to the barn. Jenny had always thought of Wayne as one of the family, and never imagined he thought of her any different.

"I like you, Wayne," she said, hoping her words didn't sound as awkward as she felt, "but more like a brother than . . . anything else."

"I can live with that," Wayne said with a slow smile.

Pushing away from the half door, he strolled down the aisle and lightly knocked Billie sideways as he passed by her.

"Oh, sorry," he said, with a tone of mock concern.

The small tomboy, who was once again dressed all in black, balled her fists and called him a name Jenny wouldn't dare repeat.

Ignoring the insult, Wayne whistled cheerfully as he went out the door.

"There's something wrong with that man," Billie declared, as she walked toward her.

"I think he likes you."

"Then why did he ask if *you* had an interest in him?"

"The same reason I received ten marriage proposals on my voicemail last night. They don't want me. They only want to win the bet. It's a game to them."

"Nick likes you," Billie said, and lifted her chin. "I've never seen him go to such extremes to marry a woman."

"Is that so?" Jenny asked, picking up a hoof pick. "How many women has he tried to marry?"

"He's never had to try to marry any. That's the point. Usually, he's surrounded by hordes of beautiful women who are all trying to marry *him*."

"Sounds like a touch life," Jenny scoffed. No wonder the man was so arrogant. He'd probably expected her to swoon at his feet like some mindless bimbo.

"What would you like for dinner?" Billie asked. "I'll cook your favorite meal."

Jenny couldn't help rolling her eyes. If Chandler thought he could get his sister to cozy up to her, he was wrong. She wasn't about to waste any of her precious time on either one of them.

"Beef Wellington," she answered slyly, knowing the meal would take hours to prepare, "with herbed carrots, mashed potatoes, biscuits, and gravy."

Billie's eyes grew wide. "I'll try my best."

Jenny laughed as soon as Billie was out of earshot.

The Chandlers could try all day, but it wasn't going to get them what they wanted.

She imagined herself getting what *she* wanted. What a wonderful, beautiful day it would be when she strolled into the Bets and Burgers Café on July thirteenth. Maybe she'd add a little swagger to her walk, like Irene Johnson.

She'd be unmarried of course, and have the biggest, brightest smile on her face—brighter than the sun. Pete would be forced to humbly declare her the winner of the bet and place the glorious, debt-defying ten-thousand-dollar check into her eager outstretched hands.

She might be the only one cheering, but she'd cheer all the way to the bank. She'd cheer when Stewart Davenport tore up the foreclosure papers. And she'd cheer when she got back home with . . . well, with Harry, for one, and . . . the horses.

Jenny frowned. There had to be other people she could invite to her celebration party.

THE LATE-EVENING HEAT bore down on the ranch with wicked intentions, leaving everyone in desperate need of a cold shower and a really good meal.

Jenny approached the picnic tables, and when Chandler turned toward her, she hesitated in midstep. Chandler's direct gaze electrified every nerve in her body. How could she ignore him when he looked at her like that?

Self-conscious, she turned her attention to her lanky red-bearded cousin who sat beside Wayne Freeman.

"Patrick, what brings you here?"

Her cousin smirked. "I heard you got someone to replace Wayne's feeble attempts in the kitchen and thought I'd come for a good dinner."

"You don't like the way I cook?" Wayne asked, a wide unaffected smile spreading across his face.

"Hate to break it to ya," Patrick told him, "but there's a reason your restaurant failed."

"Yes, there is," Wayne agreed, "but it wasn't because of the taste of the food."

"You're a chef?" Nick asked.

"Was. Past tense." Wayne shifted his jaw and looked him square in the eye. "But I'm sure your sister is a much better cook than I am."

Jenny watched Nick glance toward Billie, his expression tense. Did he doubt his sister's ability?

Patrick poked her arm. "Where's Harry?"

"He went to bed early. We had to round up the cows from the entire hillside and we're all exhausted."

"Me too." Patrick's smile faded. "The real reason I came tonight is to say goodbye. I sold my ranch to Stewart Davenport."

"*No!*" Jenny shook her head, her stomach contracted into a tight ball. "Patrick, how could you?"

"I don't have the money to keep my ranch, not in this economy."

"You don't have to go," Jenny protested. "You can stay here with us and be our new ranch manager."

She glanced at Chandler and he gave her a dark look. But wouldn't Harry prefer family over a stranger for the position? Patrick could be the answer to her problems.

"I'm sorry, Jenny, but I'm done ranching. Besides, you've taken in enough homeless cowboys." His gaze swept over Nick, Wayne, Frank, and young Josh, who sat quietly at the end of the table. "No offense, guys."

"None taken. If it weren't for Windy Meadows . . ." Wayne shook his head. "Where will you go?"

"I thought I'd head down to California for a while, lie on the beach, maybe give surfing a try."

"You're leaving?" A tight knot formed in Jenny's chest.

"First thing tomorrow."

"But this is your *home*."

"My home seems a bit empty." Patrick slouched forward. "Lately, I don't even know what it is I'm working for."

"For *this*." Jenny swept her hand toward the rich sungold meadows, pine-scented evergreens, and granite peaks stretching into a vibrant finger-painted sky. "We work for this."

"It's not enough. I want something more."

What more was there? She didn't understand.

"From now on, home will be wherever I hang my hat." A sudden gleam entered Patrick's eyes. "I want to enjoy life, not work so hard I don't know what day it is."

"Here, here!" said Wayne, lifting his mug in a toast.

"I want to wake each morning with something to look forward to," Patrick continued, "and go to bed each night with someone to keep me warm."

"Here, here!" the others at the table chorused.

Jenny's throat tightened. She thought of all the childhood memories they'd shared. Their float trips down the river. Their forts in the woods. The rope swing they used to jump into the lake. How could he just pick up and leave? If Patrick wanted someone to warm his bed at night, why didn't he just get a dog?

Drat! A tear spilled over the rim of her left eye. She hoped no one would notice, but when she wiped her cheek with her hand, she saw someone *did* notice. Double drat! Nick Chandler noticed everything.

She turned her head, spotted the large smoking tray in Billie's hands, and stifled a groan. Could the night get any worse? Jenny glanced around at the others, her stomach clenched, and braced for the next wave of disaster.

Patrick's jaw dropped. "What are we having?"

"Charcoal, by the looks of it," said Frank with a sneer.

"It's a—a roast." Billie set the tray down on the table. "It's just a little . . . well done."

"Overdone," Wayne amended. "Where did you go to culinary school?"

"I didn't," Billie said, and bit her lip.

Wayne arched his brow. "Then how did you learn to cook such a mouth-watering piece of . . . uh . . . whatever it is?"

The men laughed and Jenny looked past Billie's hard-nosed expression to the wounded look in her eyes.

Jenny knew that look. It was the same look she'd seen in the mirror after she'd been laughed at, *ridiculed*, by the men who'd placed bets at the Bets and Burgers Café six years before.

First there had been one laugh. Then another. Followed by two more until the laughter joined together like a thunderous stampede. Around and around it went, racing from one end of the room to the other, grating on her nerves and devouring every shred of self-confidence she'd ever possessed.

"*Stop!* It's not Billie's fault." She choked on her words and caught a surprised look from Wayne. "I think the temperature gauge on the oven is broken."

Billie stared at her. Jenny stared back, but instead of the young woman's difference in size and appearance, all she saw was herself.

Maybe it was because Patrick's announcement had left her vulnerable. Or perhaps it was her mind playing tricks on her. All she knew, at that moment, was that she and Billie were the *same.*

NICK ROSE AT four A.M. and discovered an urgent e-mail message from the previous day on his computer. Ten seconds later, he had his vice president at N.L.C. Industries on the phone.

"Vic Lucarelli called," said Rob. "He's not happy you and Billie took off. He thinks you're hiding her—trying to get her out of the country or something."

Nick's jaw clenched as he pictured the ruthless casino owner in his head. Wispy black hair, tanned features, beady dark eyes—-the man was exactly the type one would expect to meet in a back alley. Why his sister thought she could cheat the guy at a private game of cards, he didn't know. All he *did* know was that he had to protect her.

"Rob, did you tell Lucarelli I can get him the money Billie owes him as soon as I sell these Northwest land parcels to Mr. Davenport?"

"Yeah."

"And?" Nick held his breath and could almost hear Rob squirm during the brief hesitation that stretched between them.

"If you don't get the money within the next two weeks he's coming after you."

JENNY PULLED THE covers higher, hoping to catch a few more minutes of sleep before chores needed to be done. A few more minutes of . . .

Her heart rate doubled as she sprang straight up in the bed and glanced around the room. She was alone. Taking a deep breath, she eased back against the pillows.

She'd dreamed about him last night. As much as she hated to admit it, Nick Chandler had entered her dreams . . . and *kissed* her. She could almost feel . . . She ran a finger over her lower lip and shook her head.

So what if he was the best rider she had ever seen? She'd fallen for rodeo stars before and it brought nothing but trouble. No, she couldn't allow herself to lose focus. She needed to win the bet. She needed that ten-thousand-dollar check to save her ranch. She could not subject herself to any more of Nick Chandler's playful teasing looks or incorrigible banter.

There was no way he'd ever really fall for a girl like her. He was too good-looking, too full of himself, too determined to win her heart. Men like him couldn't be trusted. They always had an ulterior motive for whatever they did. And he was distracting her. That's what he was—a big distraction. Well, she couldn't let him distract her any longer. Harry had asked her to give Chandler a week, but she couldn't allow the handsome cowboy to stay another day.

Jenny dressed and, once outside, squinted against the bright sun as she scanned the fields.

She spotted Harry's white hair at the far end of the pasture and marched toward him, fists clenched. Harry would listen to her this time and there was nothing that dream-invading Casanova cowboy could do about it. Chandler would be off the ranch within the hour.

Jenny quickened her pace and kept her eyes on her uncle. Harry began to swing a hammer, then he clutched at his arm and staggered backward as if stung. She'd warned him about the bees by that fence.

But a man doesn't keel over from a bee sting.

"Harry?" Jenny broke into a run. "*Harry!*"

Chapter Five

NICK RAN PAST Jenny and dropped to the ground next to the old man's body. Harry wasn't moving. Ripping open his employer's shirt, he bent his head to listen for a heartbeat.

Jenny fell down on her knees beside them. "Dear God, no."

"He's alive." Nick straightened and glanced at her ashen face. "Jenny, I need your help."

At first she didn't respond. She appeared dazed, as if in shock, and he shook her hard.

Then she motioned him aside, and proceeded to check Harry's vitals. "His pulse is faint. His airway is clear, but he's not breathing. I need thirty chest compressions, like this." Jenny placed her hands together and pumped her uncle's chest. "I'll give two breaths, and then you continue the compressions."

Nick nodded and followed her lead. He'd never given

anyone CPR. When her uncle failed to respond, he wondered if it was his fault. "Should I press harder?"

"No." She lifted her head. "You're doing fine. I think he's . . . Oh, dear God, he's turning blue."

Nick glanced at Harry's marbled face, and despite the intense heat beating down upon them, an icy drop of sweat ran down the length of his spine.

"We've got to get him to the hospital." His hands pumped Harry's chest a bit faster. "The farm truck?"

"Still broken. Wayne drove his pickup into town for supplies. Yours?"

"Billie took it to buy groceries."

Jenny's face fell. "There's no other vehicles on the property. The neighbors are gone for the weekend and Harry will never make it if we have to wait for an ambulance. The hospital is forty-five minutes away."

"I can cut the time in half."

"How?"

Harry's entire body shook, startling them both, and Nick realized he was trying to cough.

"Hang on, Harry." Tears streamed down Jenny's cheeks as her uncle's eyes fluttered open. "Please, hang on."

"Sorry." The whisper hung softly on Harry's lips as his right hand inched across the ground to grasp hers.

Nick swallowed hard. He couldn't let the old man die. But what would he tell Jenny when she saw N.L.C.'s logo on the helicopter? He hit the first number on his cell phone.

"Sam," he said, his voice hoarse, "I need a chopper at the O'Brien ranch. *Now!*"

JENNY SWAYED OVER Harry's still form as the helicopter angled to the right. If it weren't for the sharp metal buckle of the seat belt biting into her middle, she'd never believe any of it was real. How could her big, strong uncle be so weak? How could they be flying, instead of driving, to the hospital in Wenatchee?

Just minutes before, the helicopter had swooped over the southern hillside, its blades whirling like a monstrous hummingbird. As it set down in the field, the propeller's wind whipped at her hair and her clothes.

Her main focus had been on Harry as she helped Nick and the pilot set him on the floor of the helicopter. It wasn't until she went to climb in with her uncle that she saw the emblem on the side door.

Jenny gasped. Let out a shriek. Involuntarily tried to step back. Instead, she tripped and fell. Landed on her butt in the dirt.

She pointed to the hateful blue-and-green spiral. "This is N.L.C. Industries' helicopter."

"It's the only one in the area," Nick said, taking her arm to help her up. "We have to go. Harry's life is on the line."

Well at least N.L.C. Industries had finally been good for something. She looked over at the hard-faced G.I. Joe look-alike at the controls of the chopper. According to Nick, it was a lucky coincidence his pilot friend, Sam Reynolds, was in town. Nick assured her that Sam didn't work for N.L.C. Industries, but the company had brought him in to evaluate the airstrip they'd acquired south of town.

Nick sat beside him, pushing buttons and monitoring data, as if they'd worked together their whole lives. Where did Nick meet him? And where did Nick learn to operate the inside of a helicopter? She didn't quite buy the fact Sam was here by coincidence but she had more important things on her mind—like the pallid complexion of her dear sweet Uncle Harry.

Her head swam and her stomach felt downright sick. Everything seemed to float around her, as if she were trapped in a terrible dream.

"Radio the hospital in Wenatchee," Nick instructed Sam. "Tell them to call Dr. Carlson."

Frowning, Jenny leaned forward and placed her hand on Nick's arm to gain his attention. "Who is Dr. Carlson?"

"Harry's cardiologist."

Jenny stared at him, openmouthed, unable to speak.

Nick gave her a swift compassionate look. "He didn't want you to worry."

"He told you? You *knew* about this?"

"It's the reason he hired me."

Her thoughts flew back to Nick's first day on the ranch. No wonder Harry had insisted they keep him. Her throat ran dry as guilt squeezed the air from her lungs. All this time she'd been trying to make Nick quit, she'd only been thinking of herself.

"Oh, God," she said, her eyelids stinging. "I'm so sorry."

TWENTY MINUTES LATER, the hospital crew carried Harry out of the back of the chopper on a stretcher and wheeled him into the emergency room. The admitting nurse told Jenny to remain in the waiting area, so she headed straight to the pay phone to call her cousin Patrick.

No answer. Had he already left for California? If he was on the road she wouldn't be able to tell him her uncle Harry was in the hospital. He'd want to know. Patrick and Harry weren't related, having come from different sides of her family, but after living next door to each other for so long, Patrick had come to think of Harry as his uncle, too.

Next she called Sarah at the bakery, thinking maybe the older woman could keep trying to call Patrick for her. But Sarah went into hysterics when she found out about Harry, and Jenny doubted she'd be much help.

Jenny hung up the phone and the familiar sterile stench trapped between the boxed walls of the building made her nauseous. She'd been in the hospital too many times for too many dying loved ones. Today the odious scent hit her harder than ever before. Harry was all she had left. What would she do if she lost him?

Nick, never leaving her side, led her over to a couch to sit down. A woman handed her a pen and a clipboard full of forms, but her vision blurred until she could hardly see the paper. *Don't cry*, she told herself. *Force it back*.

She laid the forms aside and looked up at the ceiling. A dark stain the size of a melon marred the white expanse of what could have been a perfect paint job. Why hadn't anyone bothered to wash it away or paint over it? Didn't they know someone like her would look up at the ugly thing?

Not all the nurses were attending to life-and-death situations. Some were on the phone, some were on the computer, and some were sitting around and drinking coffee. With all the uniformed staff working this day, couldn't one of them take a few minutes to remove the stain from the ceiling? *Or tell her what the heck was going on?*

Why did they all seem oblivious? Didn't anyone care? Where were the doctors? Why wasn't anyone giving her an update on Harry's condition? Were they running tests? Hooking him up to monitors? Giving him medication? The last she'd seen, Harry had still been conscious. A good sign. But when would they let her in to see him? Or have someone come out to see her?

The minute hand took a full turn around the clock before the double doors separating her from Harry opened and Dr. Carlson called her name.

She jumped to her feet. "How is he?"

"Harry suffered a mild heart attack. One of the three coronary arteries is blocked eighty-five percent and he'll need surgery to open it back up." Dr. Carlson's eyes filled with concern when he looked at her. "Did he mention any heart-related symptoms he might have had during the last few days?"

"No. He said nothing."

Beside her, Nick shifted his feet. "He's had occasional twinges of pain in his chest. Last night he said his left arm bothered him and he didn't feel well. He told me he meant to make an appointment to see you next week."

"He should have called sooner." Dr. Carlson shook

his head. "Harry's last appointment with me was three months ago. I gave him some pills to thin his blood and told him to stop working so hard. I don't suppose the stubborn old coot listened to me."

Jenny's throat constricted into a painful knot as she thought about the way Harry rose at five A.M. every morning to work the fields, mend the fences, and herd the cattle. If she'd known about his heart condition, she never would have let him work another day in his life. She would have taken away his cigars, made him rest, insisted he eat properly.

No wonder he hadn't told her. If there was one thing Harry couldn't stand, it was being babied.

"The surgery will take hours," said Nick as they sat back down. "Would you like to go for coffee, or—?"

"I want to stay."

Her mind replayed Harry's collapse in the field and for one terrified moment, Jenny wondered what she would have done if Nick hadn't been there to help. There was no way she could have lifted Harry herself, and with the ranch hands gone and no vehicle . . .

"Nick, I want to thank you for . . . what you've done. You saved his life."

"You're the one who saved him. Where did you learn CPR?"

"Veterinary school," she whispered.

He gave her a startled look. Perhaps he hadn't expected a poor country girl like her to have had much education.

"I'd planned to be a veterinarian, but I didn't gradu-ate. I came home after my third year when the money got tight. I had always planned to go back and finish, but then six months ago, my father died and I took over the ranch."

"Where's the rest of your family?"

"My grandparents and my mom . . . they're all . . . buried beneath the apple tree in the northeast corner of the property."

A fearsome ache wrenched the pit of her stomach. An ache similar to the one she'd experienced when she was very small and lost in the woods for the first time.

Her best friend, Michelle, had deserted her to run off to Florida. Her cousin Patrick left for California, and now with Harry's failing heart . . . she had no one left she could turn to. No one except Starfire, and she needed more than the companionship of a horse right now.

The pressure inside her head strained against her skull, her lungs tightened against her rib cage.

She was alone. Absolutely, *unbearably* alone.

Nick wrapped his arm around her shoulders, and she jumped at his touch. He studied her with an expression she couldn't quite place. Compassion? Sympathy? What it was, she didn't know, but when she looked into his eyes she was drawn into the silver-gray depths—and for one timeless second it was almost as if he understood her.

"Shhh," he whispered against her ear. "Let it go."

She didn't have the strength to protest. She needed to be held, even if it *was* by the man who had bet against her. Drawing in a deep breath, she collapsed against his chest.

It had been a long time since she'd been in a man's embrace. She clung to her resolve not to trust him, but

Nick's arms were warm and secure, and—at least for this one moment, she felt safe enough to release the deep, agonizing sobs she'd kept bottled up inside.

NICK STROKED THE back of her long auburn hair, and as the hour drew on, Jenny quieted. His own raw emotions flooded over him as he thought of the similarities between Harry and his father.

Both were men of integrity, rooted in their own beliefs and working as if there were no tomorrow.

"My father told me someday we'd be partners and run the largest company in the nation."

Jenny raised her head and he realized he'd spoken the words aloud.

"He spent endless days and nights designing blueprints for buildings, researching products, running the numbers." Nick paused, smiling to himself. "He said he was doing it all for me and our future business."

"He must have really loved you."

"Billie thinks so. She was jealous he didn't include her in the plans."

"Is that why she tries to be a tomboy?"

"Nah. I think it has more to do with the fact she was the only girl on my grandfather's ranch after our parents died."

"What happened?" Jenny's tears subsided and she wiped her eyes on his shirt.

Not that he minded. Her tears cooled his skin, and soothed the bitter taste of the memory. "A drunk driver hit their car head on. It happened New Year's Eve. I was ten. Billie was six."

"I'm sorry." She began to push away from him, as if realizing for the first time she was on top of him.

He continued to hold her tight. "Sometimes I wonder what my life would be like if they were still alive. The business I built is very different than the one my father planned."

"You own a business? What kind of business?"

Nick shook his head and wasn't going to tell her anything, but then reconsidered. "Manufacturer of Fat Happy Horse Treats."

"Is that how you get the horses to listen to you? With horse cookies?"

Nick grinned. "Satan loves them."

"I bet the feisty chestnut I put you on loved them, too," Jenny accused. A small smile escaped her lips but then faded as fast as it had come. "If your cookies can train horses as ill-tempered as mine, your business must make a lot of money."

Nick shook his head again. "Overhead expenses and a malicious embezzling accountant can lock up a company's cash flow for months, making it hard to get money when you need it."

"Is that why you want my land? You hope to find the gold everyone thinks is buried on my property to get a little extra cash?"

"All I want is to marry you. Is that so hard to accept?"

Jenny nodded, her face solemn. "Yes."

"Why?"

"It doesn't make sense. Why would you want to marry me?"

Nick turned her around on his lap and looked straight into her eyes. "Because you have everything that I want."

IT WAS NEARLY nightfall when Harry came fully awake.

"Hey, Harry." Jenny leaned forward in the straight-backed chair beside his bed and touched his cheek. The lines of his face had deepened and his eyes were circled by dark shadows, but at least his skin no longer resembled blueberry cheesecake. "Dr. Carlson says the surgery went well, but the nurses are all hoping to keep you here a few more days. Were you flirting with them in the operating room?"

"I'm too old to flirt." Her uncle cracked a small grin. Then his face took on a worried expression. "I didn't mean to scare you."

"Me, scared?" She forced a laugh and met Nick's eyes across the bed. "I wasn't scared. I knew you wouldn't leave me to go on the pack trips alone."

Harry glanced between them and nodded. "I want you to go with Nick."

"It was a joke, Harry," she said, careful to keep her tone light. "The pack trips aren't important."

Her uncle took hold of her arm with surprising force for a man who had been too weak to support himself earlier.

"I want you to promise me, Jenny. Promise me you

won't cancel those pack trips. Promise me you'll take Nick with you. It's the only way to save the ranch."

Take Nick? She hesitated. The time they'd just spent together did nothing to ease her distrust of the man. If anything, it made her feel even more threatened than before. But she couldn't upset her uncle while his heart was in such a precarious condition, and he waited for her reply.

"I promise," she said.

Harry turned to Nick and raised his brow.

"I won't let anyone else touch her, sir."

Nick gave her uncle's shoulder a gentle squeeze, and Harry chuckled, seemingly satisfied.

Anyone else?

Jenny had no doubt Nick would protect her from the other men on the pack trip, but who would protect her from him? She shot the dark-haired cowboy a warning look which he sent straight back at her, along with his infamous grin—and suddenly she knew.

She was in serious trouble.

Chapter Six

NICK CURSED AS he shook his deadened thumb back to life. Couldn't he even hammer a stupid nail into a post? He needed to focus. Keep his mind off Jenny. He wasn't here to feel sorry for anyone. He needed the land, needed to figure out his next plan of action. Grasping the top of the wooden post for balance, he closed his eyes and her face was closer than a coin toss away.

Her delicate brows arched upward when she was distressed. Her blue eyes darkened. Her lips parted ever so slightly. How could he think of anything else when she looked at him like that?

Jenny had been so vulnerable in the hospital waiting room. She'd needed him, needed his all-too-willing embrace. He thought he'd finally made a connection with her, tasted the beginnings of friendship. But by the time Wayne arrived at the hospital to drive them back to the ranch that night, Jenny had become quiet, withdrawn, and once again completely beyond his reach.

When Andrew's auto garage arrived a couple days later to take the farm truck into town to be fixed, his confusion doubled. How could Jenny afford the repairs?

"She sold her mother's wedding ring," Billie said, backing him into the privacy of the pantry. "You should have seen her face, Nick. Just looking at her almost made me cry. The ring's been in her family for generations and it broke her heart to let it go."

"Then why did she do it?"

"So she can drive back and forth to the hospital to visit Harry. She said as much as she loves the ring, she loves Harry more."

"If only I could find something she loves more than her land," he muttered. "Who did she sell the ring to?"

"The jeweler on Main Street."

"Then I better go into town."

"No need. While she went into the bakery to see Sarah, I bought it back for you."

Nick eyed his sister with suspicion. "Where did *you* get the money?"

"I played a few games of poker with the ranch hands the night before," Billie said, trying not to look at him. "And I did good."

"You gambled?" He didn't mean to shout but couldn't help it. "Didn't you learn your lesson with Victor Lucarelli?"

"I only did it so I can pay back Lucarelli. I thought it would be easier than waiting for you to win the bet with

Jenny, but then when she sold the ring and started to cry
... I had to use the money to buy it back." Billie placed the
intricately scrolled golden wedding band with its delicate
diamond setting into the palm of his hand. "Maybe it will
give you something to work with."

Nick closed his fingers over the ring and gave his sister
a playful poke. "Thanks, Billie. I appreciate your help."

"That's what I'm here for," she answered, smiling.

The days had dragged into the following week. He'd
hoped to find the right opportunity to give back the ring,
but Jenny spent most of her time at the hospital with
Harry. Each day he offered to go to the hospital with her
and each day she refused. Even worse was the fact that
today, the day they were to bring Harry back home, she
hadn't asked him to accompany her. She'd asked Wayne.

Despising himself and his inability to make Jenny de-
velop any feelings for him, Nick dropped the wretched
hammer he was using and trudged across the field to
bring in the horses. The menacing black storm clouds
were closing in fast and Jenny would have a fit if her beloved beasts were left out in the rain.

The first drops splattered the parched ground just as
he reached the stable. Little Josh led two horses inside,
but there were at least a dozen more that needed to come
in, including Starfire and another of Jenny's favorites, a
black-and-white paint named Apache.

"Get your sorry tails over here," yelled Frank, a halter
and lead rope dangling from his hands.

The ranch hand was trying to separate Apache from

the other geldings, but the lightning was scaring the horses into a wild frenzy.

"Need help?" Nick called, opening the paddock gate and letting himself in.

"Go that way," Frank instructed, "and try to head them toward me."

He went in the direction Frank indicated and began talking to the horses in a low, soothing voice to coax them to stand still.

"Get behind them," Frank yelled, just as Josh re-emerged from the stable. "Be careful, though. You have to whistle sharp when you go behind Apache. Make sure you whistle so he knows you're there."

Nick hesitated. "Won't a whistle spook him?"

"Nah. He's part deaf. Only a whistle will let that horse know you're behind him."

Nick knew it was standard practice to call out and touch the horse's backside as you circled around to let it know where you were, but a whistle? He couldn't remember hearing Jenny whistle when she went by Apache's rear. But Frank knew more about these horses and their special quirks than he did, so he gave a sharp whistle as he approached.

All at once Apache's right hind leg shot straight out, caught him in the side, and sent him sprawling face-first into the mud. For a moment all he saw was darkness. He wasn't even sure what had happened. Then he lifted his upper body off the ground and gasped as the searing pain in his ribs leveled him once again.

Spitting the gritty, manure-baked filth out of his mouth, he wiped his eyes just in time to see the devious smirk upon Frank's face.

"Oops. Sorry."

Hooting with laughter, Frank slapped Josh on the back. Then, despite the growing storm, the two led the remaining horses into the stable without a single bit of trouble.

The intensifying rain drenched Nick's body and chilled his skin. The strong scent of hay and manure rose into his nostrils. He was as muddy as a stinking hog. He tried to move and once again the sting of the kick jarred into his side. Coughing between thrusts of rib-slicing pain, he brought himself up onto his hands and knees.

It was clear the ranch hands didn't want his friendship. Without Harry's presence on the ranch the mean-spirited pranks had escalated into daily rituals. They'd spilled paint into his black Stetson, greased his saddle, and rigged a bucket of water to splash over his head as he entered the barn. Now this.

The reality of his situation hit him full force. He wasn't any closer to obtaining Jenny's land than he was a week ago. The ranch hands hated him, the horses hated him, and Jenny had pretty much hated him ever since he'd initiated the bet.

Why couldn't he make her like him? He wasn't one to accept defeat easily, but he didn't think staying on at the ranch would accomplish anything. Trying to win Jenny's affection was like trying to cut cubes from a solid block of ice. It just wasn't worth the effort. If he couldn't melt her heart and get her land, so be it. He would just have to find another way to pay Billie's gambling debt.

JENNY RAN PAST Frank and sloshed through the ankle-deep mud of the paddock where Nick was on his hands and knees.

"Are you all right?" she asked, and pulled on his upper body in an attempt to lift him.

"*Ow!*" he shouted. "No, I'm not all right. What are you trying to do, finish me off?"

She dropped her hands and bit her lip as he struggled to his feet. "Apache was abused by his previous owner. He always back-kicks when he hears a whistle."

Nick winced, the pain evident on his face. "No kidding."

"Looks like the guys are giving you a hard time," she said, and reached out to steady him.

"Not half as hard as you."

A twinge of guilt twisted her gut. She'd been hostile toward the man ever since his arrival despite his hard work and much-needed ranching skills. Then, after he'd helped her transport Harry to the hospital, she'd avoided him.

She'd wanted to break free of the invisible pull he had on her and distance herself from him. But now, as they stood face-to-face, she realized she hadn't distanced herself from anything. Here he was, in all his dynamic glory, covered with mud, spiteful and angry, and she was drawn to him even more than before.

"I want to help you," she shouted over the rumbling thunder.

"Leave?"

"No," she said, smiling at his bitterness. "With Harry laid up I have no choice but to keep you here."

"You don't need me," he said, the mud streaking down his handsome face. "Frank's made it clear he intends to run the ranch himself, and I'm sure Wayne will accompany you on the pack trip next weekend."

"What are you saying?"

"You win. I'm packing my bags."

"No! You can't leave."

"Why?" he demanded.

"Because I—I want you to stay."

He gave her a swift, startled look so intense it made her take a step backward. Catching her hand, he began slowly reeling her back in.

"Why?" he asked again, his tone becoming soft, luring, and far more intimidating.

"I . . ." She wished he'd let go of her. She wished she could slip away. Squirming like a trout caught on the end of a fishing line, her mind darted to and fro, desperately searching for a way off the hook. "We've got to get in out of the rain," she stammered.

"Not until you answer my question." He drew her closer. "Why do you want me to stay?"

"There are a lot of reasons. You work hard. You ride well. Harry likes you."

Nick let out a disgruntled laugh, and gave her a direct look that said he was plainly unconvinced.

"Give me a real reason."

Lightning flashed, thunder boomed, and the rain drove down in torrents. The ground shook, threatening to split apart the very foundation she stood on.

"It wouldn't kill you to admit *you* like me," he said, baiting her.

"All right. Fine," she spat angrily. "I like you. Is that what you wanted to hear?"

"Yes," he said with a grin, "very much."

The way he looked at her made her pulse race nearly as fast as the beat of the driving rain that poured down over them. Then he tugged on her hand and nodded toward the shelter of the dry buildings.

"Can you make it up to the house?" she asked.

"I hope so," Nick replied. He winced with each step, but at least he could walk.

"I'll be there in a few minutes," she said, and clenched her hands into fists as the faint strains of chortled laughter met her ears. "There's just one more thing I need to do."

Jenny entered the stable and wiped her face with a nearby towel. "Frank, you're fired."

The ranch hands were gathered around Wayne, who had missed the outdoor excitement—and as they turned to look at her, their laughter dropped off into stunned silence.

"Hey, look, I was doing you a favor," said Frank, puffing out his chest. "Chandler's no ranch manager and you know it. He just came here to win the bet. What you need is a real man."

"A real man?" she retorted. "While you and your friends are off playing cards, drinking beer, and wasting time on stupid pranks, Nick Chandler has been working his butt off. Do you think I haven't noticed who brings the cows in at night or who's been harvesting the hay? Why, he puts every single one of you to shame."

"You little fool," Frank exclaimed, his face aghast. "You're falling right into his trap."

Jenny pointed to the door. "You can pack your gear and leave."

Wayne and Josh stood frozen, staring openmouthed as if afraid she'd fire them next.

Jenny turned to Wayne and his face paled. "While Chandler and I are away on the pack trips, you will be in charge of the ranch."

"Me?" Wayne relaxed his stance and smiled at Frank's glowering face. "I guess I can be a real man from time to time."

Realizing Frank hadn't moved, Jenny gave him a little wave. "Good-bye, Frank."

"I'll get you back for this," Frank promised as he stomped away. "You just watch and see."

Jenny pushed aside Frank's threat of revenge as she climbed the stairs of the old two-story timber house. She would worry about him later. Right now her main concern was if any of Nick's bones had been broken. She stepped through the doorway of his room to find him struggling, without much success, to remove the wet T-shirt from his upper body.

"Here, let me," she said, setting her black medical bag on the table and moving forward to help him.

"I'm okay. It's just a little—" He drew in a sharp breath as she pulled the dripping garment up over his head.

"Sore?" she asked, and slung the shirt over the back of a chair.

"Yes."

"Are there any sharp, knifelike pains?"

"I don't think so," he replied, his voice ragged.

Her gaze drifted over his bare shoulders, down his finely toned chest, and finally focused on the place along his rib cage she was supposed to be examining.

"Oh, my gosh," she exclaimed, staring at the horrendous purplish black bruise on his left side.

"It's not as bad as it looks."

"To make sure there's nothing broken, I'm going to have to press on it."

She stared at the wound, her fingers hovering in midair just a mere inch away from his skin.

"Afraid to touch me?" he teased.

"No," she said, and pressed against his rib cage.

He flinched. "*Oww! Blast it all to—*"

"Sorry," she apologized.

"I'm not sure who is worse," he said, clenching his teeth, "you or Frank."

"I fired Frank," she said without looking up.

"You did?"

"Of course I did. You could have been killed." She dug in her black medical bag and brought out a roll of white bandaging tape. "I don't think anything is broken, but I'm going to wrap your ribs anyway."

As she circled his upper body, an acute sense of awareness shortened her breath and made her fingers tremble. While working on the ranch she'd seen plenty of men without their shirts, but Nick's upper torso was, well, superb, and she was so darn close to it.

"Anyone less muscled," she said, swallowing hard, "could have been seriously hurt. Still, it's probably too painful for you to ride."

"I can ride," he said, giving her a dark look. "Don't you dare try to use this as an excuse to leave me behind on the pack trips."

"But the first pack trip is this weekend. That's just three days from now. You can't possibly—"

"You promised Harry you'd take me with you."

"That was before you got hurt."

"I'll be fine. Besides, I thought you enjoyed finding new ways to torture me."

"Absolutely," she said, smiling.

Suddenly, the power went out and a loud clap of thunder shook the darkened room.

"Stay here with me," he said, hooking an arm around her waist and drawing her toward him, "and you can torture me all you like."

"Forget it, cowboy." She pulled away from his grasp and gathered her medical supplies. At the doorway she hesitated and glanced back at him over her shoulder. "Just because I like you doesn't mean I want to jump into bed with you," she warned. "I still intend to win the bet."

Nick gave her one of his sly heart-stopping grins. "Me too."

LATE THE FOLLOWING day, Jenny was outside the stable when one of the horses shied away from the roadside fence and lifted its head to send out a whinnying cry of warning to the rest of the herd.

Jenny instinctively looked over her shoulder. *Drat!* Stewart Davenport, manager of Mountain View Bank, was headed straight for her. The wheels of his monstrous, ink-black pickup spit gravel and kicked the dust into an ugly brown funnel-cloud as it barreled up the long, narrow driveway.

She dropped the wheelbarrow with a thud, spilling some of the steaming manure and old yellowed stall shavings over the side. Wiping her hands on her jeans, she cast an anxious glance up toward the two-story timber-framed house, where Sarah watched over her Uncle Harry. Then her gaze darted toward the barn, and into the crisp, golden hay fields beyond. The hum of a tractor echoed in the distance, but Nick, Wayne, Josh, and Billie were nowhere in sight.

She'd have to face Davenport alone. Taking a deep breath, she steeled herself for what was sure to be an unpleasant visit. When the bank manager made house calls it was never to chat about the cows or to sip a glass of lemonade.

Stewart Davenport climbed out of the truck, his hair slicked back, tie straight, and his cheap cologne overpowering the rank smell of the wheelbarrow of manure. Her mortgage was more than six months behind, and judging from the grim set of his jaw, he wasn't too happy about it.

"Hello, Jenny," he said, tipping his gray cattleman's hat toward her. His hard, stony expression matched the rough tone of his voice.

"Hello, Stewart," she replied, crossing her arms over her chest. "How nice to see you again—so soon. Is there anything wrong?"

"Besides the fact your ranch continues to slip further and further into debt, and you haven't returned any of my phone calls?"

"Harry was in the hospital and I—"

"I heard about Harry," he said, cutting her off. "God knows everyone hears about everyone and everything in this small town. I also heard about your bet with Nick Chandler."

"The ten thousand dollars I win from him will go straight toward the ranch debt and the upcoming pack trip money will cover the rest."

"I didn't come here to discuss your finances."

Jenny raised her brows. "You didn't?"

"You fired my cousin."

"Frank was costing us valuable money."

"You weren't paying him a salary. He worked hard for his food and board, and you threw him out on the streets."

"I'm sure he could live with you for a while, since you *are* his cousin. You don't seem to be hurting for money."

"Don't you get sassy with me, Miss O'Brien. Your

father and I had a deal. He agreed to hire Frank so I would extend his loans."

"I am not my father and you haven't kept your end of the bargain. You threatened me with foreclosure the last time you were here."

"This land would be put to better use if it were turned into a resort. Such a venture would boost the economy and make the town thrive once again. The *bank* would thrive again."

"I won't let you take Windy Meadows away from me," she said. "I will have the money I owe you by the end of summer."

"You'll need the money before that. I'm moving up your foreclosure date."

"You can't do that!"

"Frank was the only one who kept the ranch running all these years. Now that you fired him I don't see why I should give you any more time." Stewart Davenport handed her an official bank notice with her new foreclosure date stamped at the bottom.

Jenny gasped. "July thirteenth?"

The bank manager chuckled. "I thought it would make the bet more interesting."

Jenny ground her teeth. The vile man's presence made her skin crawl. The sooner she won the bet and paid her back debt, the better. More than anything she wished she had the money to pay off her mortgage completely so Stewart Davenport could never step foot on her property and threaten her again.

She had been born on the ranch. She knew every trail,

every stream, every rock, tree, and gopher hole. Windy Meadows wasn't just her home, but her *life*.

Ever since she could remember, she had been helping her father and the other ranch hands round up the cows, mend the fences, and harvest the hay. And when she wasn't working, she'd fish with her cousin . . . or go into the woods to gather wild berries for her mother's homemade jams . . . or hike up to Harp Lake to swim with her friends.

But what she loved most were the horses. She raised them, trained them, and won trophies and blue ribbons with them. There was nothing better than racing across the open fields with the wind in her hair, the sun in her eyes, and the crisp, clean vanilla scent of ponderosa pine wafting down over the mountains.

She gazed out over the golden, sweet-scented fields, the horse's heartwarming neighs calling out to her, and she couldn't imagine living anywhere else. *Ever*.

"You can't take away my ranch," she repeated, fear spiraling out of control up her spine. "I won't let you."

Davenport gave her a smug half grin. "I bet my money on Chandler."

Chapter Seven

NICK STUFFED AN extra shirt into his backpack as Billie entered his bedroom and closed the door.

"Did you search Jenny's room?" he asked, adding a pair of pants to the pack as well.

"Mission accomplished." Billie flopped down on the end of his bed. "First off, she isn't the neatest person you've met. Clothes are tossed everywhere, old bridles hang in her closet, and every flat surface is covered with family photographs."

"Sounds a lot like her tack room," he mused. "Did you find anything useful?"

"She likes men in white dress shirts. It was written in her journal. She thinks white dress shirts are sexy."

"Slim chance of wearing a white dress shirt on a ranch. Anything else?"

"She likes to read." Billie tossed a book into his lap. "Romances. Her shelves are lined with them."

"What kind of girl likes romance but doesn't date and refuses to marry?"

Billie swatted her hand at him as if he were stupid. "The kind who must have had their heart broken pretty bad in the past."

"Like when you overheard dad say girls who wore dresses were useless?"

Billie bristled. "I was only six! Besides, I barely remember him."

"You haven't worn a dress since."

Billie sprung up from the bed and circled the room. "We moved to Grandpa's ranch after that. Wearing a dress around a ranch is as impractical as a white dress shirt. If anyone should understand broken hearts, it's you. Remember when Caroline broke up with you?"

Nick's jaw tightened. Caroline. The woman who had used him to work herself up in the business world, take half his most reputable clients, and then toss him aside without so much as a 'thank you dear' on her way out. After her was Stacy, who appeared innocent enough, but had all the makings of Caroline on the inside. In fact, almost all the women he dated proved to be Caroline in one form or another. Each one taking a piece of his company with them. And his heart.

That's why when he found he couldn't pull the money Billie needed out of company funds, he chose to come out here and deceive Jenny. He was angry at Jenny for rejecting his buy-out proposals—angry at any woman's rejection since Caroline. He wanted to get back at her—

had no qualms about coming out and trying to romance the land away from her.

Until he met Jenny in person and saw how much she cared about the ranch and the people around her. How vulnerable she was when Patrick told her he was leaving and again when Harry collapsed and lay in that hospital room. She wasn't heartless and vindictive; she was crushed, and just barely hanging on.

Heartbroken. Just like him.

"Now there's a surprise. You'd never know Jenny is a sucker for romance by the way she treats me. What have I been doing wrong?" Nick studied the book cover. A man and a woman were dancing in a rose garden. "How do the men in the books make the women fall in love with them?"

"How should I know?" Billie said, throwing her hands up in the air. "*I* certainly don't read them. But maybe you should. The men have arrived for the pack trip and are flirting with her like mad."

"They're here?" Nick crossed to the window and sucked in his breath. Almost a dozen men surrounded Jenny in the yard below. "They think they can win the bet and search for the gold at the same time."

"Good luck," said Billie.

Her woeful tone reminded him of the uphill battle he was about to face. With so many others vying for Jenny's attention, when would he have a moment alone with her?

JENNY SWALLOWED THE building saliva in the back of her throat as she lined up the pack string and made some last-minute adjustments in the pecking order.

Most designated wilderness areas in Washington limited the party size of humans and animals to a combination of twelve heartbeats, but she would be taking her group into the Lake Chelan-Sawtooth Wilderness, which allowed twelve people plus eighteen pack and saddle animals. Her stomach twisted in knots just thinking about it. She was going to be up in the mountains, alone, with eleven men.

Even now, the thought of backing out crossed her mind, but she was the only one who knew the trails, could cook, *and* had medical experience in case of an emergency.

"Trust Nick," Harry said, from a wheelchair, which allowed him to be outside. "He won't let any of those men touch you."

"How can you be so sure?"

"Oh, I'm sure." Her uncle chuckled.

"And if Nick should misbehave?"

"He won't," Harry assured her. "But it wouldn't hurt to let him get to know you, Jenny. If you are ever going to love someone, you're going to have to take risks."

Heat rose into her cheeks. "I am not going to risk loving a man who only wants to win a bet."

"Can I quote you on that?"

Startled, she turned around to face a short little man, holding a pad of paper and a pen in position to write. "Who are you?"

"Alan Simms, reporter for the *Cascade Herald*."

"Did you sign up for this pack trip?"

"Yes, I did," he said, lifting his pointed nose in the air and staring at her with the brown beady eyes of a rat.

"No, you cannot quote me," she said, handing him a saddle that nearly dropped him to his knees. "And if you do write anything about this pack trip, it better be good."

"I promise," said the rat-man, giving her an unnerving grin, "it will be good."

Her uneasiness grew as Charlie Pickett, David Wilson, and Kevin Forester arrived. Hadn't she told those three seasoned cowboys she didn't want to marry them?

Charlie inherited his ranch from his grandfather, but he dreamed of singing and one day becoming a recording artist with platinum music awards displayed on his wall. He wasn't committed to Pine, and she suspected he might leave if offered a contract to go on tour.

David was quiet, a bit untidy in appearance, and his best friend was a hound dog who liked to drool all over the front porch. While she appreciated his sincerity and ability to live off the land like his grandpa, Levi MacGowan, he didn't appear quick-witted and he lacked ambition.

Kevin owned a ranch three tracts over, on the other side of the Hanson's hayfields. He shared a love of horses, something she could relate to, but he was also a fireman whose heart had been burned by his last girlfriend. Passion didn't extend past his cowboy poetry and Jenny knew he proposed only as a friend.

Ted Andrews, owner of Andrew's Auto Garage had

also laid down money at the café, but he was so obnoxious his bet didn't count. The man couldn't even ranch.

Her hands trembled as she checked off their names on her clipboard and collected their money. She should have gone over the sign-up sheet herself instead of letting Harry do it, but after coming home from the hospital her uncle needed a task to make him feel useful.

"Jenny!" Wayne hurried toward her with his hand locked on Billie's arm. "Shouldn't she be going with you? What if she has an epileptic seizure?"

Billie yanked her arm free and screwed her face into an infuriated scowl. "I am *not* epileptic."

"We're only allowed twelve people," Jenny told him. She smiled at Billie. "And she's not epileptic."

"That's not what she said when she came here," Wayne argued. "I heard she was epileptic and had nightmares."

"It is a nightmare to try to wake her up in the morning," Jenny admitted. "I bought her a second alarm clock but it didn't help. I think she needs fifty of them."

"The only nightmare around here is you," Billie shouted, and kicked Wayne in the shin.

"Ow!" he cried out, releasing her. "Jenny, you can't leave me alone with her, the little varmint's a menace!"

Jenny frowned. "You won't be alone with her. Harry and Josh will be there with you. And Sarah."

Wayne looked at Billie, who glared back at him.

"You're just afraid I'll beat you at poker again," Billie taunted.

That's not all he was afraid of. Jenny thought Wayne looked about as wary of staying home as she did about going on the pack trip, but then his expression relaxed.

"Billie, what is your full name?"

The young woman lifted her chin. "Barbara Jean Chandler."

"Big name for such a small person," he drawled. "Must go with the big attitude."

While Wayne and Billie continued to fight, Jenny spied an old man with a long white ponytail tying a weathered green rucksack behind the saddle of one of the packhorses.

"Levi, what on earth are *you* doing here?"

"Goin' on a pack trip," he said, brushing down his white woolly whiskers.

"But—" Jenny's mind whirled. "You've been exploring these mountains since before I was born. Why would you want to pay *me* to take you on a pack trip?"

"For the entertainment," he said, his eyes twinkling. "Never in the history of Pine has there been a more anticipated event, and you can be darn sure I ain't gonna miss it."

"I'm afraid you might be disappointed," she told him. "We're just going to ride up Wild Bear Ridge, camp, and ride back down again. You've already done that a thousand times."

"Yep," he said with a chuckle, "but never with a group of eleven men who are all tryin' to marry one woman. It should prove to be *mighty* interesting."

She tried to laugh. She wanted to cry. She glanced at Nick, who was loading sleeping bags and tents into the pack boxes, and her tension eased.

Despite her initial protests, she was glad the tall, dark-haired cowboy was coming along. No matter how bleak the situation, his lighthearted banter could always make her smile.

Except he didn't banter with her as they headed out over the old logging trail. He didn't even ride next to her. While she rode in front of the group, Nick brought up the rear to make sure no one fell behind.

"Quite a view," sang Charlie Pickett, riding up beside her as they crested the rocky bluff at Talon's Point, "but not half so pretty as you."

She attempted a smile, and failed, wishing she could escape and fly like the eagles circling above.

She should be happy. It was a perfect day for the pack trip. A light breeze held off the summer heat. The scent of the lush green meadow grass was remarkably fragrant. And the day was filled with sparkling sunshine. Who couldn't be happy when the sun was shining?

Me, Jenny thought, chewing her lower lip. She'd been hearing corny comments all morning as each of the men vied to ride in the position beside her on the trail. Each of the men, that is, except Nick. He remained a million miles away, at the tail end of the pack string.

By mid-afternoon she'd stopped the group at the twenty-five-foot fire tower, where they would camp for the night. Following her lead, the men dismounted, tied the horses to the hitching rail, and climbed the two flights of creaky stairs to the top. The glass windows of the timber cabin were dusty, so they went out to the wraparound deck to get a better look at the land below.

"I've never been up here," said Alan Simms, taking a camera out of his press bag.

"Wild Bear Lookout was built in nineteen thirty-eight and manned by the U.S. Forest Service until nineteen ninety-seven," she said, gazing at the town of Pine and the surrounding ranches miles below. "It's been abandoned ever since."

"Great place to see fireworks," Ted Andrews commented. "Although I see fireworks every time I look at you, Jenny."

She rolled her eyes in disgust and the men laughed.

"Fireworks have been banned this year. The area is too dry," Kevin informed them, "but this place would make a nice romantic getaway, wouldn't it Jenny?"

"With the right person it might."

"Jenny, look!" Kevin pointed into the sky. Red smoke billowed out in streams behind a single-engine plane maneuvering in a dancelike fashion across the sky.

"What in tarnation is that there fella tryin' to do?" Levi exclaimed.

"He's writing a message," Kevin told them. "The pilot is a friend of mine from the fire station."

"I see some letters forming now," said Charlie. Then he began to sing, "It says, 'Jenny marry me?' "

"The pilot wants to marry Jenny?" asked David, scratching his scruffy brown head.

"No, you imbecile. *I do*. I paid the pilot to write the message for *me*." Grabbing hold of her waist from behind, Kevin pulled her close. "Jenny, we've known each other since grade school and I figure marriage is a practical solution to both our problems. I have no money to loan you, but if you marry me, I'd be happy to sell my ranch to save yours. I need the river to water my herds, and to me, a marriage between us just makes sense. So what do you say?"

Her stomach locked down hard. If she *were* to marry, she didn't want a marriage that just made sense. She wanted what her parents had—-true love.

"Sorry, Kevin." She twisted out of his arms and darted away from him, her heart pounding.

Kevin frowned. "I've been denied."

Of course he was denied. She would deny every single one of them. Kneeling, Jenny squeezed the handle of her boot knife, and let the air exhale out of her lungs. She didn't want any of them to grab her like she was some plaything to toss back and forth. If Kevin had held her a moment longer she might have used the knife to protect herself. Especially since it appeared her appointed bodyguard wasn't going to intervene.

She glanced at Nick, who hovered toward the back of the group. He watched her, but neither smiled nor said a word. What was wrong with him? Didn't he care Kevin had his arms around her?

A short while later, Jenny drew closer to him to find out. She put eight of the horses into the preexisting ten-by-ten wooden corrals. The rest were tied to high hitchlines, which Nick set up between the trees.

"How's it going?" he asked, his focus on the leftover rope he was coiling.

"Well, the men are having fun. In spite of their numerous attempts to propose to me the pack trip appears to be a success. What do you think?"

"I'm starving," he said, finally meeting her gaze. "When are you going to cook?"

"Is food the *only* thing on your mind?"

Nick nodded, his expression innocent. "Yes."

Stunned, Jenny watched the handsome dark-haired cowboy shift his attention back to the rope. Why was he so quiet? Why didn't he smile or flirt with her like usual? She shot him a look of annoyance and stumbled over a root on her way to unload the cooking supplies.

NICK GRINNED BEHIND her back. The men were in rare form this day, and she was going to need him to step in and save her before the night was over.

Listening to all their conceit and murmured intentions had aggravated him to no end. The skywriting proposal had been especially irritating. But something snapped inside him when he saw Kevin wrap his arms around her. He didn't like it. He didn't like it one bit.

He'd also been disgusted when one of the nine other men kissed her cheek as they descended the fire-tower stairs.

But what riled his temper the most was when Charlie Pickett tried to carry Jenny into the remote ground-level equipment garage that lay twenty meters from the base of the fire tower. Fortunately, the garage door had been locked, and with a sheepish grin the music-loving cowboy set her back down on her feet.

He'd given Charlie a new song to sing when the others weren't looking, and by the time the guy rejoined the group, he was sporting a purplish blaze of color around his right eye.

Yes, she was going to need him to save her tonight, but not until she really needed it. All the other men who wrangled for her attention were making him look good. Perhaps later tonight, after they'd become more obnoxious, he would look even better.

She admitted she liked him, and from the way she kept sneaking peeks back at him while on the trail, he couldn't help but hope she'd start to show him some affection.

It would take some control on his part to restrain himself, but the longer he waited before stepping in to rescue her, the more appreciative she would be when he did. He just had to hold off for the right moment.

JENNY STIRRED THE hamburger, beans, onions, and tomatoes into a thick, spicy chili sauce. The smell encouraged the men to build a campfire in the metal ring next to the picnic table.

As soon as the coals were ready, she set in three cast-iron Dutch oven kettles stacked on top of each other. The chili simmered in the large bottom kettle, biscuits baked in the medium-sized middle kettle, and the apple cobbler she'd made for dessert cooked in the small kettle on top. The heat traveling up the towering cast-iron trio cooked each entry to perfection, and the men devoured the food as if they hadn't eaten in days.

"The way to a man's heart is good cooking—and

Jenny, my dear, this is *good* cooking," Ted Andrews informed her.

"Whose tent will *you* be sleeping in, Jenny?" asked Charlie, passing around a flask of whiskey. "There's plenty of room in mine."

"I sleep alone," she assured him, and then frowned. "Charlie, how did you get a black eye?"

"A low-hanging branch caught me by surprise near the fire tower," he said, and shot Nick a swift glance.

Jenny gave Nick a questioning look but he only shrugged and turned away to open a bag of marshmallows.

"Charlie, I can't allow alcohol to be a part of my pack trips. You'll have to put the liquor away."

"He'll put it away, all right," Ted Andrews interjected, "in his stomach. Hey, Charlie, give me some."

"I said no alcohol," she insisted.

"You can't expect a man not to indulge in a little drink while out in the wild," said Levi MacGowan, taking out his own flask. "It jus' wouldn't be natural."

It would affect their brains and make them even more eager to lay their hands on her. She looked to Nick for help, but to her utter frustration, he smiled and took a sip from the flask Levi offered him.

Drat. Levi was like a grandfather to her. And he loved his home-brewed whiskey. She didn't have the heart, *or the nerve*, to forbid him to drink after he'd paid to come on a pack trip he didn't need her to lead. And if she couldn't forbid Levi to drink, she couldn't forbid the others.

As the night wore on, the men edged closer, like a

howling band of coyotes moving in on their prey. She couldn't even go to the pit toilet without one of the men trying to follow her. What on earth was she going to do?

Levi and the *Cascade Herald* reporter sat wide-eyed around the fire as they took it all in. Nick, however, acted as if he didn't even notice.

"In case you have forgotten," she said, marching toward him, "you promised Harry you would protect me on this trip."

"You're a tough gal," Nick said with a shrug. "If anyone gets out of control, just slap him as hard as you slapped me that first day in the café."

She stared at him in disbelief. A mere slap was not going to stop this drunken band of perverts. Surely, he could see that. What did he want her to do? Beg for his help?

She was trying to return to her seat on the opposite side of the campfire when Kevin Forester reached out a big looping arm and pulled her onto his lap.

"I've got a warm seat right here for you, honey," he bellowed.

"Oh, no you don't," said Ted Andrews, tugging her away from the campfire and into the encircling shadows. "The little lady is mine."

"Let her go," said David Wilson, and he reached out to draw her back into the edge of firelight. "If she's gonna be with anyone, it's gonna be *me*."

"Why, you little bushy-haired punk!" Ted exclaimed, giving David a shove.

Kevin and Charlie stood in David's defense and suddenly Jenny found herself in the middle of a brawl.

She bent low to dodge the flurry of flying fists and pulled out her boot knife. Her protection. The one reliable thing she could always count on, besides her ranch, to keep her safe.

But before she could use it, someone whisked the knife out of her hands and fired a deafening shot into the clear mountain air.

"I'd appreciate it, men," said Nick, his hand on his rifle, "if you would keep your hands *off* my fiancée."

Nick's deadly tone, filled with more fury than she had ever thought possible, was enough to momentarily freeze everyone in their tracks. Herself included.

"Come here," he commanded, crooking his finger at her.

She moved to obey, her legs trembling, and gave him a cautious look as she reached his side.

"I must be hearing things," Ted Andrews exclaimed, narrowing his eyes on Nick. "What did you just say?"

"He called her his *fiancée*," David informed him.

All at once the men loosened up and started to laugh.

Kevin slapped his thigh. "Good one, Chandler."

Nick clicked the rifle into ready position and fixed each man with a hard stare. "I'm not joking."

"You can't possibly expect us to believe she's going to marry *you*," Ted exclaimed. "Hell would freeze over before she'd ever marry *you*."

"Yeah," Charlie Pickett added, "what about the bet?"

"Ask her," Nick challenged.

"*Are* you his fiancée?" asked Ted.

Her breath caught in her throat as all eyes turned

toward her, including Nick's. If she said no, the men would feel free to attack her. If she lied and said yes, it was possible they might leave her alone. She hesitated only a moment.

"Yes," she said, struggling to control her quavering voice, "I am Nick's fiancée."

Levi MacGowan's wrinkled blue eyes popped with excitement, and Alan Simms scribbled in a notepad as fast as his scrawny little rat-like fingers would let him.

Nick shot her a quick grin, handed her back her boot knife, and took a seat on a big overturned log.

"I still don't believe it," said Ted, louder than before. "If they are really engaged, then I want to see her kiss him."

"Yeah," Kevin shouted. "Convince us, Jenny. Kiss him."

"*What?*" she sputtered.

"It wouldn't kill you," Nick said in a low voice only she could hear.

Her cheeks blazed with heat. Of course it wouldn't kill her. What was one kiss anyway? It was simply the lesser of two evils. With one kiss she could stop the entire group from pursuing her. She met Nick's expectant gaze with uncertainty.

Drat! Taking a deep breath, she approached the log he was sitting on and placed a terrified hand on each of his shoulders. It was only a kiss, she reminded herself shakily. She wasn't selling her soul.

Chapter Eight

NICK SCARCELY DARED to breathe as Jenny drew toward him, bent her head, and brushed her sweet, whisper-soft lips against his.

It was the simplest of gestures, yet the kiss, freely given, set off an assortment of emotional charges he'd never expected.

Longing. He hadn't realized until now how much he'd longed for this moment.

Adoration. He wasn't sure if it was the helpless expression in her eyes as she walked toward him or her spitfire resolve to see the deed through, but he adored her.

Fear. He'd never felt this way before. Not even with Caroline. His heart pounded with the erratic hoof beats of a stampede gone berserk, yet his body remained paralyzed. Gone was the ability to use his arms or legs. Or his brain.

What had she done to him? All thoughts vanished from his mind except one.

He was not going to let her go.

As he slanted his mouth over hers to deepen the kiss her hands pushed against his shoulder.

Please, Jenny. The silent cry echoed between them as he moved his mouth back and forth over hers. *Kiss me.*

When she did, the wave of exhilaration that washed over him was so powerful, it nearly knocked him backward.

She tasted like a sprig of fresh mint. Invigoratingly fresh. Adrenaline-pumping fresh. Inspiring, soaring, top-of-the world fresh.

Terrified she'd pull away, he cupped the back of her head with his hand to hold her in place. This time she didn't protest, but leaned in even closer. Close enough for her heart to beat over his. Close enough for her breath to warm his skin. Close enough for her hair to touch his cheek and alter all perception of reality.

Time passed unnoticed, and when they finally drew apart, Jenny whispered, "Was that convincing?"

"You convinced *me.*"

His goal was to win Jenny's heart, not lose his own. Still, it didn't hurt to desire the woman you planned to marry. It would make winning the bet that much sweeter.

"Are they still watching?" she asked.

He looked behind her at the empty seats beside the dying embers of the fire, and smiled.

"Yes," he lied. "You better kiss me again."

JENNY AWOKE TO the loud continuous squawks of a raven as it flew overhead from tree to tree. It echoed like one of Billie's annoying alarm clocks that she slept through and wouldn't turn off. A second later, the bird's friends joined in to reply.

Wiping the sleep from her eyes, she climbed out of her sleeping bag and pulled back the canvas flap of the little green tent. And with her first step outside, stumbled right over the lumpy sleeping bag that lay straight across the doorway.

She picked herself up and peered into the face of the man who guarded her tent. Nick. He still slept, but in her stumble, she'd kicked him and the sleeping bag wriggled like a giant worm. She smiled and the previous night's events swirled through her mind.

The men had started to grab hold of her. Nick told them she was his fiancée. They didn't believe it. So she had kissed Nick . . .

Heat flooded her body from the top of her head to the very tips of her toes at the memory. She'd only meant to give him one short, light, perfectly refined kiss to convince the other men to leave her alone. It worked. After the kiss, she discovered everyone else had gone to bed.

What she *hadn't* counted on, however, was having the kiss last for *three hours*.

Later she'd started toward the tents, when Nick reminded her that the men were unpredictable perverts and might pounce on her in her sleep. If such a thing happened, he said, and he was far away and unable to hear her call for help . . . She'd shuddered at the thought and almost followed him to his tent. Then at the last minute a stray wisp of sanity saved her and she held her ground and slept alone.

Was she completely daft? Now it all became crystal clear how Nick had played on her fear to manipulate her the entire night. However, the fact he'd abandoned his own tent and slept outside to guard her anyway, just in case one of the other men decided to pay her a visit, was quite endearing.

She walked quietly down the path to the lake to pick huckleberries for the pancakes she intended to cook for their morning breakfast.

She had to admit, Nick was a good kisser. So good, in fact, that for a few brief hours he'd almost made her believe there *was* no bet and he was kissing her because he really wanted to. For the first time, she dared to wonder what it would be like to lose. If they married and Nick got his hands on her land, would he still kiss her like that?

A rustle in the bushes made her jump. A second later, Nick stepped out from behind, putting her whole body on heightened alert.

She'd hoped to have some time alone. She wasn't ready to face him yet. Her head was still wandering in a colorful fantasy world where dreams could come true—a place she hadn't been in a long time.

"Quit following me," she exclaimed.

"I'm supposed to follow you. I'm your bodyguard on this trip, remember?"

"There's no one here to protect me from. Everyone else is still asleep."

"I *know*," he said, walking toward her with a mischievous grin.

She hid her smile and moved toward the edge of the lake, where she opened a small plastic container and began to fill it with the huckleberries from a nearby bush. Two black-tailed deer sprinted away at the sight of her, and Nick bent down by the water's edge to wash his face with his hands.

The clear alpine lake, set amidst glacier-carved rocks and flowering banks of Indian paintbrush, lupines, and phlox, was one of her favorite places. Farther back, towering ponderosa pines and noble fir led up to a steep stony ridge where one mountain rose majestically above all others. The sheer rock face of its jagged peak was illuminated with a brilliant purplish-orange glow in the early morning sun.

Nick let out a long, appreciative whistle.

"Everyone is in awe of Mount MacGowan the first time they see it," she said, trying to keep the conversation light. "Old Levi will spend hours telling you how it was named after his ancestors. The back of his property borders the other side of the lake and leads all the way up the mountain."

"I've never seen anything so beautiful."

She cast him a quick glance. He was looking at *her* and not the mountain. Did he really think she was beautiful?

"That rocky cliff over there," she said in an awkward effort to redirect his gaze, "is Granite Pass. There's a cave on the far end about a quarter of the way down."

Nick came to stand close beside her. Too close. His

male scent, mixed with the rough leather of his brown rodeo jacket, reminded her how good it felt to be wrapped in his arms next to the campfire.

"This is Harp Lake," she said, and gestured toward the shimmering blue-green expanse beside them. "Some say you can hear the sound of harps when the wind blows across the water."

Nick leaned in even closer and blew lightly into her ear, making her spill some of her berries.

"Have you ever heard it?" he asked.

"No. Only selected people can hear it."

"Selected people?"

"Legend has it," she explained, closing the lid of the berry container before she spilled more, "the lake is protected by angels. When you come to the lake with the one you love and hear the music from the angels' harps, it means you are destined to be together forever."

"Do you know anyone who has heard the harps?" Nick asked, smoothing back a loose strand of her hair.

"My mother heard it. She was engaged to marry someone else when she met my father here. She came to tell him she couldn't see him again. Then she heard it . . . the faint strands of nearly a dozen harps . . . She looked into my father's eyes and she knew *he* was the one she was destined to marry."

"Just like you are destined to marry me."

"Nick, I wouldn't marry you if you were the last man on the trail."

He chuckled as he took her fingers, raised them to his mouth, and began to kiss the tips.

She swallowed hard. "I wouldn't marry you if I were beaten and thrown to the wolves."

Letting go of her hand, he reached for her waist and pulled her into the circle of his arms.

"I wouldn't marry you even if—"

A sudden gust of crisp, fresh air fluttered breezily down the mountains, making the lake water ripple. She could have sworn she heard . . . her breath caught in her chest as she stared out over the lake and then up into Nick's silver-gray eyes.

"Would you marry me if you heard the harps?" he asked, his voice dangerously soft.

Stumbling out of his embrace, her heart hammered and her mind raced. It wasn't possible. Was it?

"Not all legends are true," she sputtered, and broke into a run as she headed back to camp.

Nick watched Jenny's hasty retreat and laughed. He hadn't stepped foot in a church since his parents died, but if it helped to have Jenny think a higher power had destined them to be together, he'd play along with it.

He glanced back over the sparkling blue lake. What on earth could have produced the sound of harps? It had to be the rock formation on the opposite shore acting like a whistle.

For no angel would let him near her.

THE MEN WERE in a somber mood as they helped Jenny roll the tents and repack the saddlebags and pack boxes. Not even "cowboy cappuccino" or talk of the gold mentioned in her great-great-grandfather's journals could perk them up. Everyone was quiet. Everyone, that is, except Nick, who whistled cheerfully as he bounced around camp grinning from ear to ear. The other men grimaced and muttered cutting remarks about him under their breath.

Jenny was thankful the men were keeping to themselves. She needed to sort out the crazy thoughts whirling about in her head.

Did she really hear the harps? She tried to take deep breaths. Tried to remember the bet and why she'd accepted.

It was ridiculous to feel this way over a man, yet she couldn't help herself. With his dark hair hanging over the collar of his blue flannel shirt, his dancing eyes, and flirtatious smile, he was absolutely irresistible. If the legend of Harp Lake was true, was she destined to marry him after all?

Her thoughts returned to the first time she'd attempted marriage, and her father's voice pierced through her memories as loud as if he were standing beside her.

"What kind of man is over an hour late to his own wedding?" George O'Brien demanded, pacing back and forth in front of the altar for the hundredth time.

"He'll be here soon, Dad." Jenny ignored Reverend Thornberry's doubtful expression and glanced toward the church door in anticipation. "Travis *loves* me."

Travis. Just saying his name made her go weak in the knees. She couldn't help herself. From the moment the handsome rodeo star pulled into town, twirling his brown cowboy hat around on his fingers, she had been smitten.

"He might have overslept," she said, calmly pushing a loose spiral of her long auburn hair away from her face. "He's had to put in some very long hours lately."

Her father glanced at his watch and let out an impatient groan. "Well, the guests aren't going to stand around and wait all day."

"Neither am I," Reverend Thornberry interjected, looking down the bridge of his nose at her.

She gazed out over the murmuring crowd, who had dressed in their Sunday best and were starting to suffer from the extreme summer heat. The men were loosening their ties and mopping their brows with handkerchiefs, while the women fanned themselves with the paper wedding programs they had been handed at the door.

"You're right," she conceded. "I'll just run across the street to his room above the café and see how much longer he's going to be."

"That might not be a good idea," her father said hesitantly.

"I'll go," her cousin Patrick volunteered.

"I don't want you to embarrass him," she said, shooting them all a smile. She smoothed the white satin and lace skirt of the bridal gown that had once belonged to her mother. "I'll go. Travis has either overslept or . . . oh, Dad, what if he is sick? I hope he didn't catch that flu that's going around."

"He could be sick," Patrick admitted. "But it wouldn't be from flu. I heard he drank quite a bit at his bachelor party last night. I bet he has a nasty hangover."

Worrying over his well-being, Jenny gave the wedding guests a small apologetic smile and hurried across the street faster than she had intended to.

The Bets and Burgers Café was nearly empty due to the fact that most of the townspeople were waiting at the church to see her get married. With a quick wave to Pete, she made her way up the stairs to the second floor, where Travis had been able to rent a room for half the cost of one at the Pine Hotel. The café was a historical landmark from the gold-mining era and did not have an elevator. Usually she didn't mind, but today the ascent was making her breathless.

Just as she placed her hand on the doorknob to her fiancé's room a low groan sounded from within. *Travis.* Maybe he *was* sick. Her heart flipped over with concern. She should have come sooner. Why did she wait so long?

Yanking the door open, she rushed inside.

"*Jenny.*" Travis's eyes widened as he scrambled to pull the tangle of bed sheets over a squirming array of glistening naked body parts. "It's not what you think."

At the moment she wasn't thinking at all. She simply stared, her mind strangely numb and detached from what her eyes were seeing in the dimly lit room.

Travis's handsome face was beaded in sweat, his disheveled dirty-blond hair sticking out in different directions. His chest was heaving as if he had difficulty breathing . . . or had just engaged in intense physical activity.

The curvaceous lump beside him wriggled beneath the sheets, and let out a sound that was half giggle, half scream.

Another scream resounded off the walls, one she recognized as her own.

"Jenny, what are you doing here?" Travis said, struggling to sit up.

What *was* she doing here? Travis was obviously not the man she had thought him to be.

"In case you forgot," she said, forcing the words to her lips, "you were supposed to meet me at the church over an hour ago to get married."

"He changed his mind." The feminine voice belonged to Irene Johnson, who suddenly popped her curly blond head out from beneath the sheets and erupted into another giggle as she snuggled into Travis's side.

It was bad enough that he was in bed with another woman, but *Irene Johnson?*

"Travis, how *could* you?" Her eyes pricked with tears as hot as burning coals. Stepping back, she turned to leave.

"Jenny, *wait.* Let me explain."

"*Explain?* How can you possibly explain why you are in bed with that barroom tramp on our wedding day?"

"She doesn't mean anything to me," Travis said, waving his hand. "*Trust* me."

Irene's gloating Barbie Doll face fell, and the young woman who had been her high-school rival sprang off the bed, dragging the sheets with her and leaving Travis's naked body exposed.

"How could I ever trust you after betraying me like this?" Jenny demanded, averting her eyes.

"We can still be married," Travis said, grabbing his pants up off the floor.

"Do you honestly believe I would be stupid enough to marry you now?"

"Your father already signed the papers giving me the southwest section of the ranch to build our home. If you don't marry me, those hundred acres are still mine."

"Obviously you didn't read the fine print," she said, her temper flaring at the realization Travis cared more for her land than he did for her. "If we don't get married, the contract becomes null and void."

Not waiting another moment, she stepped over the threshold and left the room. Her legs trembled as they raced down the stairs. Tears blurred her vision and her throat felt as though it had been sliced. Her stomach began convulsing in alternating waves of sickness and panic.

She had *trusted* him, told him she *loved* him, and was willing to spend the rest of her *life* with him. Didn't it cross his mind she might come looking for him when he didn't show up at the church? Didn't he think to lock the door?

She squeezed her eyes shut, trying to block it out of her mind, but the image of Travis lying beneath the twisted sheets with Irene came forth with razor-sharp clarity. His voice haunted her as well.

"Trust me . . ."

What was she to do now? She couldn't possibly go back to the church and face all those people. She *couldn't*.

As it turned out, she didn't have to. By the time she made it down the stairs, a large crowd of the men had occupied the tables in the café and ordered drinks. Every eye was upon her as she burst into the room. But her gaze wasn't on them. Not really. Her gaze was on the chalkboard, which had Travis's name written between hers and Irene's.

Later she'd learned the other men had taunted him. Said he'd lost his edge with women. Bet Travis couldn't get Irene to sleep with him that night as a "last fling." Travis took the bet.

But she suspected as much as soon as she saw the chalkboard. And when the men staring at her realized she knew what had occurred, their faces were not filled with guilt or compassion or concern for her feelings. Unbelievably, the men at the café laughed. They *laughed*, as she stood there in the middle of the room . . . and felt like the loneliest person in the whole world.

From that day forward she let it be known she was through with all of them. Never, for as long as she lived, would she *ever* make the mistake of trusting a man again.

But she'd made that vow before Chandler came along and before she'd heard the harps.

Did fate have another plan in mind?

WHEN THEY ARRIVED back at the ranch late in the afternoon, the men from the pack trip said their good-byes and left.

"What's the matter?" Billie asked with a frown. "Didn't they have a good time?"

"They didn't get what they wanted," Jenny informed her.

"What did they want?"

"*Me*," she said with amusement.

Nick, wearing a big smile, playfully mussed the top of his sister's hair as he passed by.

"*Someone* got what they wanted," Billie observed.

Heat rushed into Jenny's cheeks and she tried to change the subject. "What were you and Wayne doing by the river?"

Billie and Wayne exchanged a suspiciously guilty look and then Wayne walked away, carrying the two shovels they'd been using in his hand.

"We were digging up some river rock to—" Billie paused. "I'm not going to lie, Jenny. We were searching for the gold."

Jenny smiled. "Did you find any?"

Billie shook her head and gave her a rueful grin. "No."

"If you had found gold," Jenny asked, "what would you do with it?"

"We'd give it to you, of course. But if you were willing to share, Wayne said he'd pay a lawyer to help regain visitation rights with his two girls, and I—I owe a casino owner in New Jersey a chunk of change."

"Are you and Wayne friends now?"

Billie shrugged. "Wayne bet I couldn't muck out all the stalls before noon and I proved him wrong and made him help dig for gold."

"What if you lost?"

"I would have had to pay him twenty dollars. But he also said he'd buy me a steak dinner for my effort."

"Steak dinners aren't cheap. Maybe you should have let him win."

"Would you let *him* win?" Billie asked, and nodded in Nick's direction.

Jenny hesitated. Of course, she wouldn't let him win. Just because she'd lost her head for a few moments beside the campfire didn't mean she'd lost sight of the prize. But what if she found a big fat gold nugget to solve her financial problems? Would she let Nick win the bet if the money no longer mattered? The truth was, she no longer knew. She'd vowed not to trust any man, but could she trust herself?

Her inability to remain indifferent to Nick Chandler's charm was humiliating enough, but on Monday, the stupid local newspaper had a photo of her kissing Nick on the front page.

Drat! The rat-man had a camera. Appalled, she threw the paper to the living room floor. She hadn't noticed anyone taking her picture. She hadn't been aware of anything while Nick kissed her.

She picked up the newspaper again. The caption beneath the photo read, "Chandler's Chances Looking Good." She scowled with disgust as she rapidly skimmed the article.

Is the bet over? Newcomer Nick Chandler took ten local men by surprise Saturday night when he announced Jenny O'Brien was his fiancée. Jenny reportedly confirmed his statement and then proceeded to smooch with Chandler for the remainder of the evening.

"I tell you, it was disgusting," Ted Andrews stated morosely. "She could have had me."

"She looked happy," David Wilson commented.

Immediately after this announcement all bets at the Bets and Burgers Café rose in Chandler's favor seven to one.

The floorboards creaked behind her, making her turn with a start. Nick hovered in the doorway, an identical newspaper in his hands.

"It will take more than a kiss to get me to marry," she said, jumping to her feet.

"How about a dozen kisses?"

Suppressing the urge to smile, she shook her head and made her way down to the stable.

Wayne, Billie, and Josh were in the tack room when she arrived, huddled together in a tight circle.

"What's going on?" she asked, unable to see over their shoulders.

The circle quickly broke apart, but not before she saw the newspaper Wayne stuffed behind his back.

She gasped. "I can't believe you're reading that trash!"

"A picture is worth a thousand words," Wayne teased.

"You know," said Billie, "if you marry Nick, then we can be sisters."

"I'm not marrying anybody."

Josh pulled the newspaper away from Wayne. "It says right here you're engaged."

"I am *not* engaged," she shouted in a strangled voice.

Her nerves were raw. They were invading her private space. The tack room was supposed to be the one spot she could go to hide. Now there didn't seem anywhere to hide. Nowhere at all. The walls of the stable were conspiring to close in on her, and escaping into the open fields wasn't an option. Josh waited for his weekly lesson and she was obligated to meet him in the outside arena. Another place of suffocating fences and gates, and tight penned-in enclosures.

Harry sat in a chair by the arena to watch and when she drew near she saw he was reading . . . *Drat! Not another newspaper! Where did they all come from?*

Josh Hanson followed her out of the stable and pulled three more papers out of his newspaper delivery bag. "The bet is great for my paper business. Karen Kimball says if I keep selling this many papers I'll be the richest kid in town."

Harry chuckled. "I see the pack trip was a huge success."

"No, it wasn't," Jenny said, and counted to ten to try to control her temper. "The phone has been ringing off the hook. Every single one of the men who booked pack trips for the next three weekends has now canceled. We needed that money, Harry, and now there's even less time before the bank deadline. What am I going to do?"

"You could ride." Harry flipped the newspaper over and showed her a large ad.

Peering over his shoulder she read, "The annual Pine Tree Dash is to be held on Saturday, July sixth at the East Creek Fairgrounds in Pine."

"You won the race three years ago, and the money's good."

"But Starfire isn't performing as well as he used to. I'm afraid his age is catching up with him. I'll need to find a new horse to ride, one I can train within two weeks."

"You can do it," Harry said, looking healthier than he had since his collapse. "You're a great trainer. And if you win, you'll have half your bank debt covered a week before the deadline."

"Thanks, Harry," she said, hoisting herself up on to Starfire's back. That's exactly what she would do.

She would find a horse to win the race.

Chapter Nine

NICK LOCKED THE door to his room. His cell phone stated he'd missed ten messages from N.L.C. Industries. As he returned the call, he brought up the company's files on his computer.

"Where have you been?" Rob Murray demanded.

"On a pack trip," Nick replied. "What's wrong?"

"Victor Lucarelli says your two weeks are up. If you don't come back to New York to talk to him, he's flying out there to Pine."

"I'm on my way," Nick told him. "If anyone found out I'm the CEO of N.L.C. Industries it could ruin everything, especially my relationship with Jenny."

"You have a relationship now? I thought you considered her a business deal."

"She's a person," Nick answered, "and I'm trying to find a way to pull off this deal without Jenny getting hurt.

"I don't see how that's possible if you take her land.

Speaking of getting hurt," Rob said, dropping his voice. "Are you bringing Billie back with you?"

"No. She'll be safer here, out of Lucarelli's reach."

"Let me know when you get to the airport and I'll send you a car," Rob said loyally, "and maybe a bulletproof vest."

Nick attempted a laugh, but it stuck in his throat. Nothing about his situation was funny. Lucarelli had friends in places no law-abiding citizen would dwell.

Still, he didn't think the man would hurt him as long as there was a chance to recoup the money Billie cheated him. More than flaunting his power, Victor Lucarelli wanted his hundred grand.

Nick arranged his airfare and shut off his computer. Once in New York he'd talk to Lucarelli, tell him about his plans to sell the land parcels to Davenport, and ask for more time.

But what could he tell Jenny? He tried to think of a plausible explanation for his required upcoming absence. He thought of their kiss instead.

Damn. He didn't want to go. He didn't want to leave her, even for a day.

WHEN JENNY FINISHED with Josh's riding lesson, Nick took her arm and led her down the path toward the river. She didn't question him but walked along by his side. It was clear from his expression he had something important to say.

"I have a confession to make," said Nick, taking both

of her hands in his. "I've been running a small business from my computer at night."

"Yes, you told me, your company manufactures Fat Happy Horse Treats—pleasing to horses of all temperaments," she said, careful to keep her tone light.

She'd expected to evoke a smile or a teasing response, but his expression remained serious. Whatever he had to tell her must be worse than she thought. She held her breath and waited for him to begin.

"I need to leave the ranch for a few days to meet with my suppliers in New York."

He was leaving? Her mouth fell open. It was the last thing she'd expected.

"Well," she said, and shrugged to suggest she didn't care one way or the other. "Do what you have to do."

Nick studied her face for a moment and then placed a finger beneath her chin. "Can I have a kiss good-bye?"

She hesitated, afraid if she granted his request, she'd give away too much of herself, too much of her crazy mixed-up feelings. Stopping by the edge of the churning, cajoling river, she turned to face him and lifted her brows. "Why?"

"Because I would like my fiancée to give me one."

This time he *did* grin, and she relaxed, and smiled back at him. "I am *not* your fiancée."

"You told the men on the pack trip you were," he teased.

"Only to stop them from harassing me and you know it."

Nick took a small black-velvet jewelry case from his pocket and lifted the lid. "I bought you a ring."

Jenny gasped, stepped back, and then forward again for a closer look. "Where did you get that?"

"The jeweler told me it would make a fine engagement ring. Legend says this ring once sealed the union of two lovers who knew they were destined for each other the moment they heard the harps at Harp Lake. I thought it would be perfectly fitting, since we—"

"You *knew* this was my mother's ring when you bought it," she accused. "Billie told you, didn't she? Why, this is just another ploy to win the bet!"

"Is it working?"

She shook her head. "This ring wasn't just my parents' engagement ring, it was the engagement ring of my ancestors for four generations. Shamus O'Brien, my great-great-grandfather who found the gold, had it custom designed."

"It's one of a kind," Nick agreed, "like *you*."

"I never would have sold it," Jenny continued, "if I wasn't so desperate to fix the truck and visit Harry at the hospital. I was afraid of losing him, but to lose this ring . . ." Her voice cracked. "I don't think you understand how much this ring means to me."

"Oh, I think I *do*," he said, removing it from the box and slipping it on her finger.

"We are *not* engaged." She looked from the ring on her left hand to the cunning expression on Nick's face.

"Then if you want to keep it, you'll have to pay me."

"How?" she choked out. "You know I have no money."

"You can start," he said, and leaned closer to give her a direct look, "by giving me a kiss."

Drat! He was manipulating her again, but only if she let him. She didn't have to kiss him. She could send him off to New York without so much as a peck.

But something within his expression, something within the innermost depths of his eyes, something even in the way his body stood, made her draw toward him as if pulled by a magnet. She'd wanted to kiss him again ever since the kiss by the campfire, and if it was *her* choice to kiss him, then he wasn't really manipulating her, was he?

Nick met her halfway and she closed her eyes as his warm mouth connected with her own. It was actually terribly sweet of him to have bought the ring back for her, even if he *was* using it to bribe her.

She ran her fingers through the back of his dark silky hair, and pulled him closer. She'd never been kissed like this. With so much intensity and unbridled emotion it seemed she would transcend the universe.

She knew the kiss should end, yet couldn't push him away. Not when he'd be gone for who-knew-how-long, and she'd be left alone on her ranch like the days before he'd come. She didn't want to be alone anymore. Perhaps if they stayed like this, time would stop and they'd never reach the dawn of a lonely tomorrow.

Apparently, Nick felt the same. The fiery kiss spiraled out of control, and the flames of desire soon reached a fevered pitch so high that it threatened to combust into a whole new level of intimacy.

Nick groaned low in his throat as he suddenly tore his mouth away from hers, squeezed her tight in his arms, and buried his face in her hair.

"You *are* what I want."

He pulled his head back and looked at her as if he expected her to repeat the same words back to him.

But she couldn't. As much as she wanted to, her fragile heart wouldn't let her.

"I really like the way you kiss me," she admitted.

"Well," Nick said, smiling at her, "that's a start."

NICK TOOK THE glass elevator to the top floor of the Winner's Luck Casino in Atlantic City, New Jersey. Upon entry into the private quarters, he forced himself to reach forward to shake Victor Lucarelli's hand. The casino owner ignored the gesture and motioned for him to take a seat opposite him at the square marble table in the center of the room.

A rivet of alarm fastened to Nick's optimism as he pulled his hand back to his side and sat in the stiff-backed chair. This was not going to go well.

"Two weeks are up," Lucarelli barked. "Do you have the money your sister owes me?"

Nick's mind worked on multiple levels to seek an answer to satisfy the gruff wispy-haired businessman, but there was only one word he could reply.

"No."

Lucarelli's dark eyes narrowed. "If you don't have the money, then you can't protect her. I *will* make Billie pay."

"I could give you three twenty-acre land parcels in Pine worth far more than the amount Billie owes you,"

Nick offered. "I could also give you the small airstrip my company purchased just south of the town."

Lucarelli stood up and laughed. "What would I do with a bunch of useless land parcels on the other side of the country?"

"You could open a casino. The locals there love to bet."

The forty-year-old man, dressed in his fine black business suit, paced in front of the array of mirrors lining the marble-columned wall. "When I heard you and your sister flew to the foothills of the Cascade Mountains I did some research. Pine is barely a spec on the map. You need a magnifying glass to see it. With a population of six hundred and ninety-seven, I'd be better off opening a casino for wood ticks. Why in the world would a fellow businessman like yourself spend time out there? What is it you hope to accomplish?"

"I plan to sell my land parcels to Stewart Davenport, the bank manager in Pine, who has a personal interest in developing the area. But he won't take my land unless I gain the title to an adjoining piece of property owned by a stubborn rancher woman."

Lucarelli nodded as if he understood. "Women can be a nuisance. So you are trying to convince this woman to sell and then you will have my money?"

"Yes. That's why I need more time. There are other men who are trying to thwart my negotiations with the young woman."

"Of what interest is her land to them?"

"They think there's a gold mine hidden on the property."

"Gold?" Lucarelli sat back down in his chair.

"It's just a rumor," Nick assured him.

Victor Lucarelli's entire countenance warmed and he offered Nick an outstretched hand. "I'll wait a little longer."

"Thank you," Nick said, and with a silent sigh of relief, he rose, anxious to head toward the door.

"One minute, Chandler," Lucarelli called after him.

A big six-foot-six solid muscle of a man crossed his arms over his chest and blocked the exit. Lucarelli's personal bodyguard. Nick stopped, his stomach tight, and turned back around to meet Lucarelli's gaze.

"Just so we're clear—you have two more weeks. If you don't have my money by then, with interest, perhaps even some *golden* interest, I'll expect payment of a different kind."

"What else could I give you?"

Victor Lucarelli smiled. "N.L.C. Industries."

JENNY FINISHED THE last of her chores for the day and was wandering aimlessly around the paddock, thinking of Nick. The ranch seemed empty without him. Quiet. Too quiet.

She was about to go into the house to check on Harry, when Wayne and Billie emerged from the barn with shovels and several large window screens tucked under their arms.

"What are you doing?" Jenny asked, catching up to them.

Billie and Wayne exchanged a nervous glance and Jenny clapped her hands together and laughed.

"Are you going back down to the river to pan for gold?"

Billie nodded. "Wayne says the screens will allow us to sift through the sandy river bottom."

"Can I come?" Jenny looked at Wayne. "Unless, of course, the two of you want to be alone . . ."

Wayne gave Billie a side glance and grinned. "Why would I want to be alone with her? I'm only bringing Billie along because her eyes are closer to the ground than mine. I figure I can use her to spot the gold."

"I'm not as short as you make me out to be." Billie lifted her chin. "I'm five foot three—and a half."

"Yeah, that half inch makes a big difference," Wayne teased.

"Better than being a beanpole like you."

Jenny took one of the screens and followed them down the path to the edge of the river. The same place Nick had brought her to propose. Of course it wasn't a real proposal. He was merely bribing her for a kiss. She smiled at the memory, and all the warm fuzzy feelings it aroused.

"I think today is going to be my lucky day," Billie said, shoveling a mixture of sand and pebbles onto her screen.

"Because you are wearing your lucky color?" Jenny asked, splashing barefoot into the river beside her. She eyed the black cutoff shorts and unflattering black T-shirt Billie was wearing. "Don't you have any clothes that aren't black?"

"Nope."

"Why not?"

"Black complements the way I feel." Billie shot a quick glance at Wayne and added, "Most of the time."

"Maybe I'll have to start wearing black if I don't get the money I need to pay my bank debt," Jenny mused, picking up a rock and turning it over in her hands.

"You'll get the money," Wayne said, "if you win the bet."

"If she *doesn't* win the bet, Nick will take care of her," Billie argued. "She can still have a ranch."

"But maybe not *her* ranch," Wayne countered.

"She could have a husband."

"Or a lot of heartbreak."

"Babies," Billie said, splashing water at him.

"Crying and more heartbreak," Wayne said, splashing Billie back.

"She could have a great sister." Billie smiled. "Like me."

"That last part is really debatable," Wayne teased.

Jenny waved their arguments aside. "I think I found something."

Billie and Wayne drew close, and Jenny held up a small rock the size of her thumb. The sun's rays sparkled off the gold flecks, mesmerizing each of them for several long seconds.

"This could be the answer to all our problems," Billie whispered.

"Only a fool would say that," Wayne said with a wide grin.

"Why?" Billie asked, reaching her hands up to touch the glistening marvel.

"Because this is 'fool's gold,' " Jenny explained, realizing her mistake. "See the tiny crystals? Real gold does not form crystals."

"Are you sure?" Billie persisted. "Maybe we could take it into town and have it evaluated by a professional."

"I'm sure," Jenny said, handing the rock over to her. "This is iron pyrite."

But for one glorious moment, she'd hoped as much as Billie that they'd hit it rich, stumbled on a miracle, or been rewarded with a stroke of luck. For the first time, she'd hoped she'd found a way to save the ranch . . . *without* winning the bet.

NICK TOOK THE train from New Jersey to his office in New York and spent the next three days juggling client meetings and paperwork he'd put on hold during his absence.

He'd talked to Jenny a couple times on the phone, but the tiny Northwest town of Pine seemed so very far, far away.

Collapsing into a chair, he stared at the bottle of victory champagne sitting on the end of his desk. A bottle he'd vowed not to open until he gained hold of the O'Brien land. *Jenny's* land.

Before he arrived in Pine he'd thought a quick marriage to put his name on the property deed, followed by a quick divorce would force her to sell. Now he hoped he could work everything to his advantage *without* a divorce.

How could he keep Jenny *and* save his business? He rubbed his temples, unable to decide on a strategy. Was his business even *worth* the tension stiffening his spine?

For the entire first ten years of his life Nick had listened to his father talk of nothing but the company they would build together. A company bigger and better than any other in the nation. His father skipped baseball games and family outings in order to draw up plans. After his death, it seemed only right for Nick to exert an equal effort to turn those plans into a reality.

Now for the first time he wondered why. Did he think it would bring his father closer to him? Nick didn't feel close to anyone. He felt . . . alone.

He missed Jenny. Missed sparring with her. He'd never known flirtatious combat could be so much . . . *fun*. He missed watching her vivid expressions, missed the emotion behind her words, missed the way she cooed to her horses.

He missed the ranch, too. New York City made him claustrophobic after working in the wide-open fields these last few weeks. He wished he could draw in a deep breath of fresh air from the shadow of the mountains. Wished he could smell the rich, welcoming scent of the pine trees or taste the crystal-clear water of the surging alpine river. After walking the streets of New York again, he even longed for the smell of the cow pasture.

He imagined himself back at the ranch, with Jenny by his side, and a tranquil sensation of utter contentment stole over him. No wonder Jenny loved the place.

It felt like . . . home.

JENNY STARED AT the phone in her father's office, each unanswered ring twisting her stomach in knots. Just another creditor demanding to know when they'd get their money. How could she speak to them when she didn't have any answers?

She still needed to pay Harry's hospital bill. The insurance didn't cover much and the doctor's fee was higher than she'd expected. Perhaps if she had stayed in school and become a veterinarian, she wouldn't have a pile of unpaid invoices on her desk.

Jenny ripped open the top envelope and discovered another offer from N.L.C. Industries to buy her property. She was just about to toss it into the trash when she stopped to see the monetary figure they had in mind. Not enough, she thought as she tore it in two. It would never be enough to make her give up the land she loved.

Frustrated, Jenny left the room and made her way down to the stable.

"Hey, big boy." She leaned over the half door of Starfire's stall and patted his sleek brown neck. "Who's the most handsome fella in the whole barn? You are, aren't you? Yes, you are."

"I'd give anything to have you talk to me like that."

Recognizing the voice, she spun around, and a surge of excitement slammed into her chest at the sight of Nick's smiling face. Why, it had been downright *dull* working on the ranch this past week without him there to trail after her, tease her, and tempt her to think traitorous thoughts.

Nick gave her a searching look. "Did you miss me?"

Why did he always have to be so darn direct? If she said yes, it would reveal too much, and if she said no, he'd know she was lying.

"We all missed you," she said. "The chores have backed up and there's a lot to do around here."

"Is that all I am to you, another pair of hands? You could tell me I'm handsome to make me feel better."

Suddenly, a forceful nudge broke them apart, and Starfire nibbled her cheek.

Nick arched his brow. "Somebody's jealous."

"No," Jenny said, smiling. "Just hungry. Can the second most handsome fella in the barn help me feed the horses?"

Nick grinned. "Only if you'll tell me how to become your number one."

Never leave. Jenny gazed into his eyes but couldn't say the words. Couldn't tell him how bright the sun was shining inside her heart because he was near.

Instead she shrugged. "Well, Starfire is a hard guy to beat."

NICK TRIED NOT to trip over the piles of presents cluttering the back entry into the house. Boxes of chocolates, dried flowers, stuffed animals, and balloons Jenny had received from the other men while he was away. Most of them looked untouched, but he was irked by the fact she hadn't thrown them away.

What could he give her? He'd bought back her mother's wedding ring, but the gift wasn't original. She'd more than likely remember her mother when she wore it instead of him.

Jenny was different from other women he knew. She wouldn't be swayed by jewels, pretty clothes, or sweet pillow talk. She didn't crave riches, fame, or power. She'd be satisfied just to keep her ranch and have the money to pay her bills month to month.

What could he give her to warm her heart and bring him a step closer to win the bet?

He noticed she didn't have a dog. Harry said they'd had a collie a while back named Rusty, but the dog ran off one night and never came back. Maybe he could buy her a puppy? Except a puppy wouldn't do her any good at this point and she might complain he'd given her another mouth to feed.

What gift, other than money, could he give her that she'd both love and need? A shrill whinny sounded from the stable and he smacked himself on the head.

A horse for the upcoming race.

Chapter Ten

FIVE DAYS LATER, Jenny loaded three of the pack animals into the trailer to take to the midweek auction. The three horses to which she was least attached. They weren't worth much, but she hoped to get enough money to buy a decent horse she could train for the race.

Nick, Billie, and Wayne were eager to go with her. The following day was the Fourth of July and the whole town of Pine was sure to be bustling with celebratory events. She felt bad about leaving Harry behind. That is, until she discovered Sarah Gardner was coming over with an apple pie.

"Are you going sweet on her?" Jenny teased.

"Me, sweet? Never. A real cowboy doesn't go sweet on anyone," her uncle replied. "Can I help it if the woman is attracted to me? She sure can cook, though," he mused, "and she can tell the funniest stories you ever did hear. Why, once she said . . ." He broke off, chuckling. "Well

. . . you better get going if you're going to find a horse at the auction."

"You *are* going sweet on her," Jenny said, and placed a hand over her uncle's heart. "Could be a side effect from the attack."

"Could be," Harry admitted with a grin.

WHEN THEY ARRIVED at the East Creek Fairgrounds several horses were already in the main arena with prospective buyers looking them over. Jenny caught sight of a beautiful dapple gray western quarter horse, and after helping Wayne unload the pack horses from her trailer, she wandered over to the mare for a better look. Nick and Billie followed her.

The horse had exquisite conformation, not to mention a beautiful gray mane and tail. Its eyes appeared bright and alert. The mare's teeth were good. Its feet were sound. The strong, muscular quarter horse would make an excellent addition to any barn. An easy sell for the owner. The price tag to a horse like this should have been advertised in magazines. Why would someone want to sell this magnificent animal at an auction?

Just then, the gray mare turned, enabling Jenny to catch a glimpse of the other side of its face.

"*Oh*," she said, drawing in her breath.

An enormous scar zigzagged across the cheekbone from the mare's nostril all the way back to its ear.

"The animal's worthless," a man muttered, drawing his wife away. "Only good enough for the slaughterhouse."

Jenny scowled. People like that didn't deserve a horse. Leaning forward, she caressed the dense, lumpy tissue. Outer beauty wasn't everything.

"She's eight years," said a bearded man with deep-set eyes. "Could use a bit more training, but she's been in good health since the fall that ripped open her face."

Jenny walked around to inspect the mare's legs. "Is she fast?"

"Very fast," the owner boasted. "Kastle beat Kevin Forester's horse, Blue Devil, in a race over the weekend."

"Kastle," she repeated, noting the auction flyer he handed her spelled the name with a *K*. *Nice name*. Fitting for the horse's large size.

She gave Kastle a gentle pat. This was the one. She couldn't explain it, but somehow, deep in her heart, she just *knew* this was the horse she'd been searching for. The horse she could ride right into the winner's circle of the Pine Tree Dash.

"I'll make you a deal right now," she said, unable to hide her excitement. "I'll trade you three excellent pack horses—"

"No trades," the man said, cutting her off. "I want cash."

"How much?" Nick asked over her shoulder.

"She goes to the highest bidder."

Jenny walked back to her own horses but her gaze kept straying toward the big gray quarter horse.

The bidding at the auction block began an hour later. She was fortunate all three of her pack horses sold early, although she didn't get as high a price as she'd hoped.

Still, it had to be enough to buy Kastle. She and Nick were recounting the money when Billie ran toward them.

"The bidding for the gray horse is about to start."

Jenny squeezed the thick wad of bills in her hand and took a seat between Nick and Billie in the outside auction arena.

"Where's Wayne?" Jenny asked, glancing around.

"Busy looking at tractors." Billie searched the entranceway. "He said he'd be here soon."

Billie's aloof expression turned to one of hope, making Jenny smile. It was clear the tomboy was attracted to the sandy-haired ranch hand and didn't quite know what to do about it.

Wayne, on the other hand, had been giving Billie more attention than he'd given any woman since Michelle left, but still only treated her like a pal.

"If he doesn't meet us here, he'll catch up with us in town for lunch," Jenny assured her. "I told him we'd eat at—"

She broke off distractedly as Irene Johnson stepped up behind Nick's chair and began to knead his shoulders with her fire-engine-red fingertips.

"Hi, handsome," Irene purred as Nick turned his head. "What are you up to?"

"Just placing some bids," he answered. "Jenny, do you know Irene?"

"Yes," she said, her body tensing as she eyed the blond-haired vixen. "*Everyone* knows Irene."

Nick gave her a curious look and then glanced over his shoulder at Irene's saucy expression and lifted his brows.

"It's a small town," Irene confided, leaning down and waving her over-stuffed bosom next to his face. "Jenny and I went to the same school, joined the same clubs, got engaged to the same man . . ."

"You were never engaged. *I* was," Jenny said, glaring at the woman. "You just slept with him."

"You were engaged?" Nick stared at her, as if he wanted to ask her a thousand questions and didn't know where to start.

She averted her gaze. "It was six years ago."

"I didn't know you were engaged," Nick said, his voice lacking the usual deep confident edge. "What happened?"

"The poor guy got cold feet before the wedding and came running to me," Irene said, raising her voice to a near shout.

Jenny narrowed her eyes on the blond witch, who was deliberately trying to cause a scene, and clenched her fists in her lap. She wanted to spring from her chair and deck the woman but she'd already made a fool of herself in public twice before. She didn't want to do it again. No, as much as it killed her, this time she wouldn't be impulsive. She'd hold on to her dignity.

"Better get back to your own seat, Irene," Billie warned, "or they'll mistake you for an old mare and start auctioning you off."

"Very funny." Irene scrunched her nose and withdrew her hand from Nick's shoulder. "Catch you later, Nick, if you're free."

Jenny waited for Nick's reply but instead of responding, Nick pointed toward the front of the auction block.

The gray quarter horse with the large zigzag scar was brought out and the auctioneer started the bidding at three thousand dollars. Jenny raised her hand. So did four others and the bid was raised to five thousand in less than a minute.

"It's going too fast," she muttered.

"One of the other men just backed out," said Billie.

"The bid is being raised to six thousand. Are you going for it?" Nick asked.

"Of course I am." She raised her hand.

"Another man backed out," Billie reported, and craned her neck to look around. "The bid is down to you and two others."

"Do I hear six thousand? Do I hear seven thousand?" the auctioneer called.

Jenny bit her lip as the two men bidding against her raised their hands. She raised hers as well.

"Do I hear seven thousand, five hundred?"

She held her breath as she raised her hand once again.

"Only one man raised his hand," Billie told her. "He looks like he has money. He's wearing a suit and tie."

Nick glanced at Jenny. "It's the bank manager."

Jenny turned her head toward the back of the crowd, where Stewart Davenport stood. He didn't have a good reputation with animals. He didn't ride. He didn't even own a barn. Why would he want Kastle?

She gasped. "Davenport wants to stop me from entering the race."

"Eight thousand. Do I hear eight thousand?"

The bank manager watched her, and when their gaze

met, he smiled. She couldn't let that devil of a man buy Kastle, but she had no choice. "It's over," she said, her voice choked. "I don't have any more money."

Suddenly Nick raised his hand and the auctioneer took his bid.

"What do you think you're doing?" she exclaimed, as the bank manager backed down.

Nick took out his wallet. "Buying a horse."

"How could you do this to me?" Jenny cried.

He knew she wanted this horse and to buy it right out from under her wasn't just mean, it was painful. Maybe he thought if she didn't win the money from the race, she'd be forced to marry him. Well, she wouldn't. She could never marry anyone who would deliberately hurt her.

Pushing out her chair, she ran out of the arena.

NICK JUMPED UP to go after her, but Stewart Davenport stopped him.

"Are you out of your mind?" the bank manager demanded. "Why did you bid against me?"

"Jenny needs that horse for the race."

"And you plan to give it to her? If she wins the money she needs to pay her bank debt, we'll never get our hands on her property!"

"If I give her the horse that wins the race, we will."

"You're losing it, Chandler. You're losing it for both of us, not to mention your sister. I thought you wanted to win the bet you made with Miss O'Brien. If Jenny wins the race, she'll wave a fond farewell and never look back. You'll lose her, the bet, the land. Everything. Is that what you want?"

Nick put a hand on his shoulder. "Sometimes going in the opposite direction is exactly what you need to do to get ahead."

"You're crazy, Chandler. Don't say I didn't warn you."

Nick pushed him aside and hurried out of the auction area to find Jenny. He might be crazy, but he was determined to give her the horse to win her heart. It had to work.

Because he could not fathom a fond farewell in his future.

JENNY HAD ALMOST made it back to her horse trailer in the parking lot when Nick caught hold of her wrist, and spun her around to face him.

"Why are you so upset? I bought the horse for *you*."

"I can't accept her," she said, shaking off his hand.

"Why not?"

"I refuse to be indebted to you. I already owe you for buying back my mother's wedding ring. I don't want to owe you for this, too."

"Agree to marry me and you won't owe me anything."

Her heart leapt at his words, but her head focused on the fact that Nick wanted to win the bet as much as she did.

"You can't buy me, Chandler," she warned, "no matter how much money you have."

"I'm not trying to buy you. The horse is a gift. You accepted presents from the other men," he reminded her.

Jenny thought of the stuffed animals, candy, and flowers she'd received and planned to donate to the hospital.

"Those gifts didn't cost eight thousand dollars. Where did you get all this money from anyway? It must be nice to be able to lay down ten thousand here, eight thousand there . . ." Her voice cracked and her eyes began to sting. "I bet you don't know what it's like to want something and not be able to get it."

"As a matter of fact I do," he countered, drawing closer. "After my parents' death my grandfather raised me and put a roof over my head, but there wasn't any extra money for college. I spent my summers traveling around the rodeo circuit winning the money I needed to go to school and start my own business. I needed to grab the bull by the horns in more ways than one."

"What are you saying? That I don't know how to 'grab the bull by the horns' to get what I want?"

She inched away, her pulse quickening, as he moved in on her, closer, and closer, until his face was directly in front of hers. She could see each individual eyelash framing his intense silver-gray eyes. Feel the heat of his breath on her face. Smell the fresh leather scent clinging to his clothes.

"You won't even *admit* what you want," he said, taunting her.

"Which is?"

"*Me.*"

"You think too highly of yourself, Chandler," she said, her voice rising as she forced herself to step away from him. "What I *want* is to save my ranch. Just watch as I grab the horns on your arrogant bull-head and win the bet on July thirteenth!"

Nick's superiority faded and an earnest expression crossed over his face, as he reached a hand out to her. "Jenny—"

The sudden change stopped her in her tracks. "Yes?"

"Please take the horse."

She wished he wouldn't look at her like that. As if he adored her and had only her best interests in his heart. It broke her concentration and made it harder for her to stay mad at him. The catch in his voice didn't help either.

Her gaze fell on the horse trailer, empty inside, with nowhere to go except back home again. A home that could be signed over to someone else within a fortnight if she didn't win the race.

"All right," she said, and a smile escaped her lips. "But there must be something I can give you in return."

She expected him to ask for a kiss, or a date, or if his arrogance returned perhaps he'd dare to ask for something more . . .

"Your boot knife," Nick said, brushing a strand of her hair away from her face and hooking it behind her ear.

"No, not my knife. I need—"

"I'll protect you," he promised. "Trust me."

Jenny swallowed hard. What he was asking for was much more than a steel blade. Could she really rely on him? She wavered indecisively for a full minute before bending down to remove the boot knife hidden beneath the bottom cuff of her jeans.

"I trust you," she said, and placed the knife in the palm of his hand.

THE BETS AND Burgers Café was not Jenny's first choice for a place to eat lunch, but Nick, Billie, and Wayne insisted. She had to admit the chicken wings with honey-barbeque dressing were better than she remembered. Afterward, the waitress cleared their plates and Pete Johnson, the café owner himself, drew toward their table.

"How much do we owe you?" Nick asked, drawing out his wallet.

"Nothing. Your lunch is on the house," Pete said, his little round face beaming. "I really appreciate the amount of business you two keep bringing into my restaurant."

"It's not intentional," Jenny told him, scanning the room, which was even more crowded than before.

Faces everywhere were turned in their direction and excited murmurs circled around them. It reminded her of the day she'd stormed in with the broom and first met Nick. She smiled at the memory now, relishing the way he'd openly challenged her and then pulled her tightly against him and kissed her. When would he kiss her again? Tonight? When they were alone?

The moment Pete left, Wayne cleared his throat and rose from the table. "Billie and I are headed toward the fairgrounds, but don't rush. We might take a detour or two along the way."

"There's lots of street vendors," Billie added, jumping up from her seat. "Maybe we'll buy some fireworks."

Jenny recalled Kevin saying fireworks were banned this Fourth of July due to the dry forest conditions, but Billie was already out the door. That left her alone at the table with Nick.

"What was his name?" he asked in a low voice.

"Who?"

"The guy you were engaged to."

"It doesn't matter," she said, squirming in her seat. "It was a mistake."

"I'm glad to see you're wearing *my* ring," Nick said, leaning back in his chair.

"It was my ring to start with," she reminded him.

"Yes, but I bought it back for you. Now it symbolizes the engagement of five generations of O'Briens."

"We are not engaged," she whispered, and glanced at the men next to them, who were trying to listen in.

"Then why are you wearing it on your left hand?" he challenged.

Suddenly self-conscious, she slipped her hand under the table and out of sight. "To make everyone else *think* we are."

His lips twitched into a subtle grin as if he didn't believe her.

She looked at the delicately scrolled golden band with its intricate diamond setting and tried to suppress the impulse to think of it as a real engagement ring. She would *not* allow him to win the bet. No matter how good he kissed.

"Heard you gave her the gray mare," Levi said, wobbling on his cane as he made his way beside them. "Is it true?"

Nick nodded. "True."

"How could you give her the horse?" another man asked. "If she wins the race, she won't need you. You'll lose the bet and I'll lose all the money I placed on you."

"I never asked you to bet on me," Nick said, arching his brow.

A chorus of men's complaints erupted around them, including the words "love-struck softie" and "yellow-bellied loser." A moment later, half the people filed out of the building.

"Well," Nick said, glancing at her. "I guess I'm officially branded a loser."

"You are *not* a loser for giving me the horse," she protested. "I won't let them think that."

"The only person whose opinions matter to me is *you*."

Jenny's heart ripped in half. Not only had he given her the horse she wanted, but he'd sacrificed his reputation for her, and her father had always told her a good reputation was very important to a man. Something he took pride in. There was no egotistical pride on Nick's face as she looked at him now. Only a sweet tenderness that rocked her senses.

He wouldn't win the bet, but she couldn't let the other men mock him for helping *her* win. She had to do something.

Jenny chewed on her bottom lip while considering a plan of action. She'd had enough lessons by now in manipulation to see how it worked. But would it work on Nick? If the other ranchers were ever going to treat him with respect, she needed to help him get his reputation back. But how?

The idea came to her in a flash as she glanced at the silver rodeo buckle on Nick's belt. *The rodeo.* The annual Fourth of July amateur rodeo was being held at the fairgrounds that very afternoon.

Her heart leapt into her throat with excitement. She had to convince Nick to enter at least one of the events. He didn't need to win. He just needed to do fairly well for the other men to admit he was a real man after all.

"You know, there's a rodeo at the fairgrounds later today," she began with a devious smile . . .

Chapter Eleven

Nick followed Jenny out of the café and listened distractedly as she rambled on and on about the amateur rodeo at the fairgrounds that afternoon. He'd seen enough rodeos in his life to be fairly bored of the event, but if it made her happy, he'd take her.

His thoughts strayed once again to the fact Jenny had been engaged. Wayne had mentioned she'd been jilted, but he didn't know she'd been jilted by a man she planned to *marry*.

How could she have said yes to a man who would readily dump her for the likes of Irene, and not say yes to *him*?

Two hours later, Jenny sat next to Nick in the bleachers of the fairgrounds arena as the calf roping got underway.

"He's really good," she said, nodding to the wrangler on horseback.

"Not *that* good," Nick said with a frown. "He took too long, and leans too far over in the saddle. He'll never win trying to rope a calf like that."

"And I suppose you could do better?" she asked, hoping he'd take the bait.

"Of course," he said with a grin. "I *did* ride professional rodeo."

"Oh, I forgot," she said, feigning innocence. "Then again, that was a long time ago."

"What's *that* supposed to mean?"

"I bet you couldn't do it now." She cast him a sideways look.

"Of course I could."

"I'd like to see you try," she said, mocking him with her tone.

"I don't have a horse."

"You can ride Kastle."

"I don't know if that horse is fit for rodeo."

"You aren't making excuses, are you?" she teased.

"I have a horse you could borrow," said Kevin Forester, coming up behind them. "His name's Blue Devil, and he's a blue roan quarter horse that ain't seen defeat."

"I bought a dapple gray named Kastle this morning. The man said the mare beat Blue Devil in a race last weekend."

"That was on a straightaway," Kevin told them. "No horse can beat Blue Devil inside an arena. If you ride him, I'll split the prize money with you. I'd ride him myself except I took a fall from a ladder at the fire station two days ago and sprained my wrist."

"Thanks, Kevin, but I don't think Chandler here has what it takes to make those kinds of moves anymore."

Nick's face flashed with insulted pride as he squared his shoulders and gave her an indignant look.

"I'll ride," he said, taking her challenge. "What's the next event?"

"Steer wrestling," Jenny said, unable to suppress her smile. "Show me how to grab the bull by the horns."

NICK SWALLOWED HARD as he rose from the bleachers and went down to the registration booth. Did he still have the skills a rodeo demanded? What if he couldn't do it? What if he got himself gored while trying to impress her?

"Either you are as good as you say you are, or you're gonna die," Wayne said, following behind him.

"Thanks for the pep talk."

"No problem," Wayne replied with a sidelong grin.

Kevin and Wayne stood on the platform behind the starting gate as Nick mounted Blue Devil and patted the horse's blue-gray neck.

"One of the rodeo clowns is going to be your hazer," Kevin informed him. "He'll force the steer to run in a straight line next to you, but you'll have to do the rest."

Nick took another glance across the arena, where Jenny and Billie sat in the crowded stands, and then over to his left, where the steer was trying to break out of his pen. A series of snorts and grunts issued from its nose and mouth, none of them friendly. The animal scraped the door with one of its horns and Nick had the distinct impression it was trying to sharpen the weapons . . . just for him.

Taking a deep breath, he called for the steer and Kevin tripped the lever opening the spring-loaded doors. The large ugly beast burst from the chute. The rodeo clown rode swiftly behind. Nick had to wait for the distancing rope fastened around the steer to break before he could race Blue Devil to catch up with them. Instinct took over. Instinct he'd developed from years of experience from both rodeo and his grandfather's ranch.

Leaning over the side of the galloping horse, Nick grabbed hold of the steer's horns and slid out of the saddle. The black beast shook its head and Nick knew he couldn't let go. He was too close. Close enough to smell the stink in its hair. Close enough, if he wasn't careful, for the beast to stick its horn into him like a skewer.

Using all his strength, he dug his heels into the dirt. A brown cloud of dust enveloped them. Went up his nose and into his mouth. Didn't matter. He'd spit later.

He gave the large head a quick twist, and then, keeping his hold on the far horn, he put the steer's nose in the crook of his left elbow and threw his weight backward. The steer squealed, but it also became unbalanced, enabling Nick to wrestle the formidable six-hundred-pound animal to the ground.

Thunderous applause broke out over the stadium as all four of the steer's feet shot upward.

"Unbelievable," Kevin exclaimed, running out and

gathering Blue Devil's reins. "Your time was under five seconds."

"Not bad, Chandler," Wayne said, slapping him on the back, "not bad at all."

IN THE STANDS, Jenny and Billie spontaneously hugged each other, and then jumped up and down clapping like mad. The crowd stamped their feet, making the stands shake beneath them. Several men who had been at the Bets and Burgers Café stood nearby hooting and whistling their approval.

"He can't be all bad, if he can wrestle a steer," one man proclaimed.

"He may have broken the record for fastest time," said another.

"I wouldn't doubt it," a third man replied. "He sure does have quick reflexes. Still, not sure if he should have given up that horse."

"Giving me the horse doesn't guarantee I'm going to win the race," Jenny told them. "It's going to be a tough competition."

"You're right," the last man agreed. "I have a cousin entering the Pine Tree Dash, and I'm betting he wins the race."

Everyone in the stands agreed. Except one, but Jenny kept her opinions to herself.

Nick and Wayne were following Kevin Forrester to his trailer to see his other horses when Jenny drew near with Billie on her heels.

"Geez, you must really like her," Wayne said, shaking his head. "You wouldn't find me wrestling a steer for a woman's attention."

"That's what separates the men from the boys," Billie said, coming up behind them.

"I ain't no boy," said Wayne.

"Prove it," Billie challenged. "Team roping is next and Nick needs a partner."

Wayne looked at the small young woman, whose favorite clothing color had recently lightened from black to blue. Then he looked at her brother.

"I do need a partner," Nick said, his expression earnest, "a friend I can trust."

Nick placed a special emphasis on the word "friend," and Jenny held her breath. It was important for Wayne to accept Nick's offer of friendship if the ranch was to be a success.

Beside her, Billie squeezed her arm. Jenny took one look at the tomboy's taut face and realized Billie was eager for Wayne to accept her brother for reasons of her own.

Wayne took the pack of cigarettes he kept tucked away in the rolled-up sleeve of his T-shirt, and without a word, tapped out a cigarette and lit it with his lighter. First inhaling, and then letting out a stream of smoke, he gave Nick an appraising look.

"I'll ride with you," he said finally, and reaching out, he clasped Nick's hand in a firm shake.

Jenny could hardly stop smiling as Nick and Wayne mounted the horses Kevin was letting them borrow. As they waited their turn, she climbed up on the fence beside Nick, leaned forward, and gave him a kiss for luck.

"If I win this event," he told her, his eyes shining, "I want you to promise to go to the Fourth of July dance with me."

"Nick, I don't dance."

"You'll learn."

"I don't even own a decent dress."

"I'll buy you one."

Jenny hesitated. She didn't have any intention of going to the dance. Dozens of bet-wagering men asking her to dance was not her idea of a good time. But the chances of Nick winning two events in a row were slim, even with Wayne's help. And Nick was in such a good mood she didn't want to ruin it by fighting with him.

"All right," she promised, "but only if you win."

"Each cowboy carries one rope and is allowed three throws," Billie said as she climbed up on the fence beside her, "and the roping team that went out right before Nick and Wayne was assessed a five-second penalty for roping only one hind foot instead of two."

Nick and Wayne gave each other a nod.

Jenny knew they would do well. After all, this team event originated from cowboys working on the ranch. To treat injuries, change brands, or brand new stock, the cowboys had to be quick and skilled in roping animals.

As soon as the steer's nose cleared the chute, Nick, who was the designated "header," left the box first, dropped a looped rope over the steer's horns, and turned the steer away from Wayne, who was the designated "heeler." Wayne then threw a rope to catch the back legs and time was called when both ropes were pulled tight and he and Nick turned their horses to face each other to "shape the steer."

"How many seconds was that?" Jenny asked excitedly.

"I don't know, but it had to be less than seven," Billie said, clapping.

The announcer came over the loudspeaker proclaiming a time of six seconds and the crowds went wild.

"I think they won," Billie shouted.

THE FAMILIAR RUSH of adrenaline pumped through Nick's veins as the boisterous roar from the crowd deafened his ears. In the past, he'd always ridden in the rodeos for the money, but now that he was riding for pleasure, with Jenny, his sister, and friends by his side, he found he actually enjoyed it.

After he dismounted, Jenny ran up and threw her arms around him. He picked her up and swung her around, giving her a kiss. He was thrilled to be able to do that. She was opening up to him, and kissing him and holding his hand as if she were truly his. She'd even stopped calling him Chandler and had begun using his first name, something he didn't even think she was aware of.

"I'm glad you hooked the horns and not me," Wayne said with an easy grin. "I wonder what Frank would say about your 'ability' if he saw what you did today."

"Frank was in the stands," Kevin said, taking the horses reins. "He bet against the two of you and lost a lot of money."

"He was always all talk and no action," Wayne admitted. "Chandler's a better ranch manager than him any day."

"You can really ride," Kevin said.

"Thanks," Nick said in appreciation.

As they began to walk away, he glanced at Jenny, at her satisfied expression, and stopped in his tracks.

This was why she had goaded him into entering the rodeo. He didn't care what others thought about him, but apparently, *she did*. He remembered the concern in her eyes at the café when he'd been branded a loser, and the resolve on her face when they'd entered the rodeo arena.

Why, she'd even used some of his own tactics to get him his reputation back. Perhaps she was learning how to play the game after all.

Suddenly Jenny's smile fled, and her whole demeanor changed as she became fixated on something behind him.

"What's the matter?" Nick asked, spinning around.

"He's here."

"Who?"

Nick followed her haunted gaze to the brown-haired man in the red rodeo jacket and knew the answer before the name left her lips.

"Travis Koenig."

"Is *that* the man you were engaged to?" Nick demanded.

Jenny nodded. "Do you know him?"

"Yes," he said, cursing silently. "I know him."

Travis Koenig was notorious for picking up women in every state along the circuit. The rodeo star had even tried to hook *him* up with a date once or twice.

"Let's leave," she pleaded, tugging on his hand, "before he walks over to us."

Nick followed her through the crowd, his mind tormented with unanswered questions.

Why was it that after all these years, Jenny couldn't face her ex? And that Irene could still get her so angry? Was she still in love with Travis?

Just when he thought he couldn't be in more trouble, Alan Simms, the pesky little man from the pack trip who worked for the *Cascade Herald*, jumped out in front of him and snapped his picture with a camera.

"Congratulations on winning the rodeo, Nicholas Lawrence Chandler."

Nick bristled. The reporter used his middle name. He hadn't told anyone in Pine his middle name for fear they'd put his initials together and learn his identity. Had the reporter investigated his background?

"Tomorrow morning your picture will be on the front page of every newspaper across the country," Alan Simms continued.

His gut clenched. "Why? Is the steer I wrestled famous?"

"No, but *you* are, and everything a high-profile CEO like you does is newsworthy."

The man knew who he was. Nick cast Jenny a startled glance, reached for the reporter's camera, and missed.

The tiny man shot him a devious grin, and scurried backward through the crowd.

No! His mind screamed in anguish. He couldn't let the man get away. Simms would reveal his true identity and all he had worked for would be lost. Jenny would be lost. He pushed through the crowd after him, caught a quick glimpse of his face, and was almost upon him when the smug reporter suddenly tripped over Billie's outstretched leg.

"Oh, I'm so sorry," Billie exclaimed, bending down to scoop up the camera that had fallen to the ground. "Let me help you."

The little man let out a high-pitched squeal as she opened the side of the digital camera, let the SD chip fall to the ground, and squashed it with her boot.

"Good work, Billie," Nick said, catching his breath.

"I can still print the story," said Simms, and with an odd little twist to his lips he added, "You can *bet* on it."

"Go right ahead," Jenny said, lifting her chin, "and don't forget to mention that Fat Happy Horse Treats are the best horse cookies around."

Nick caught Billie's worried glance as the reporter brushed off his pants and disappeared back into the crowd.

"Rat-man is up to his sneaky little tricks again," Jenny said, scowling. "Although the story he prints may bring in new customers for your little business and allow it to grow into something really big. Wouldn't that be nice?"

Nick barely heard her. Alarm bells were ringing in his ears, and the hairs on the back of his neck were standing on end.

Perhaps he could bribe the editor in chief to shelve the story. He glanced at his watch. It was four thirty and the bank closed at five.

"I need to go talk to someone," he told Jenny, releasing her hand. "Can you and Billie stay out of trouble for a few minutes without me?"

"I think we can handle it," Jenny said, smiling.

Five minutes later Nick came to the end of the wooded path connecting the fairgrounds to Main Street and walked into Mountain View Bank to get the money to bribe the newspaper editor.

"I'm sorry, I can't help you," the bank teller told him. "The credit cards you handed me have been denied."

"That's impossible," Nick said, his gut clenched. "Rerun them through the system again."

"Sir, I *have* rerun them. Twice."

"Just call this number," he said, taking a business card out of his wallet, "I'm sure that—"

"It's not my problem," the bank teller informed him. "You'll have to make the call yourself and come back when your accounts are in order."

Nick began furiously punching in the number to N.L.C. Industries and barked at the secretary in his office to put Rob Murray on the line.

"What the hell is going on?" he demanded when his second in command finally answered. "When my personal accounts were denied, I tried to access the company's accounts and was told that the funds were unavailable."

"We're out of money, Nick." Rob's voice sounded hollow, filled with remorse. "Lucarelli placed a few calls to our top clients and told them we couldn't repay our loans. Several of them canceled future orders and our finances plummeted. There's nothing left."

He snapped his cell phone closed and squeezed it hard. Lucarelli had promised to give him two more weeks, but it looked like he was positioning himself to move in for the kill. It seemed an impossible triangle. Jenny, Billie, N.L.C. Industries. No matter what he did, he feared that in the end he would have to give up something very close to his heart.

The cost to his finances had already been great. He'd used the last of his personal savings to bet Jenny the ten thousand dollars in the café. Billie had used her poker earnings with the ranch hands to buy back Jenny's mother's ring. His salary at the ranch paid for his airfare back and forth to New York and a few other day to day expenses. He'd sold his blue pickup truck as soon as they arrived at the auction so he could afford to buy Kastle. And after all that, he didn't have any money to convince the newspaper editor to drop the story that would alienate Jenny from him once and for all. Unfathomable.

He spoke again with the bank teller, and she directed him to Stewart Davenport's private office.

"I need your help," Nick said, removing his hat and twisting the rim in his hands.

"After the way you treated me this morning at the auction?" Davenport asked. "I can hardly believe my ears."

"Please," Nick begged.

Chapter Twelve

NICK WIPED THE sweat off his brow as he made his way into the house. He'd managed to strike a deal with Davenport. He didn't like the terms. But for the present moment it gave him a small amount of cash.

The editor of the *Cascade Herald* couldn't be swayed, but Nick figured he and Billie would get up early, and with more than a little luck, buy up all the town's newspapers before anyone saw a copy. The action would buy him a day at most, but the truth remained—he had to tell Jenny who he was.

He needed to find the right time and the right place. He needed to carefully plan out the words he would say to her so she wouldn't find him offensive. Except, he'd thought about it all evening while doing chores and still didn't know how to start.

It was late. He didn't expect anyone else to still be up, but as he made his way across the kitchen, a dim light and the distinct murmur of the TV slowed his pace. Sticking his head through the living-room doorway, he spotted Jenny sitting cross-legged on the couch, her eyes glued to the screen.

"Did you know there's a millionaire who attended a charity ball in Boston who has the same last name as you?"

"I . . ." Sudden apprehension pricked his spine. *She had been watching the news.*

"He's a CEO."

Nick's muscles tightened, and his mouth ran dry. "Did they mention the name of his company?"

"I didn't catch it. Drat! I wish Billie hadn't broken my radio. I hardly know what's going on anymore."

He would have to remember to thank Billie later. Too bad she didn't break the TV while she was at it.

"Was the guy good-looking?" Nick asked.

"I only saw him in the background, but it doesn't matter."

"What doesn't matter?"

"Rich corporate people who attend those events are all snooty, egotistical show-offs."

"Maybe," Nick said, carefully considering his words, "the CEO donated a vast amount to the charity."

Jenny smirked. "If he did, it was probably for a tax write-off."

"Maybe he believed he could help."

Jenny smiled and shook her head. "You've been watching too many movies."

"The CEO may even be a nice guy, like . . . me," he said, boldly testing the waters before he went on.

Jenny gazed up at him with her bright blue eyes and let out a laugh.

"You said it yourself. I have the same name as the CEO. What makes you so sure I'm not him?"

"That's simple. You work. Men like that rich CEO have other people run the company for them. They just sit at their pretty little desks in their fancy glass-windowed offices, toasting the success of their latest business ventures with bottles of champagne."

Nick swallowed hard, realizing this was *exactly* what he had done. In the past. Before the company's finances nose-dived through the floor and disintegrated.

"But the biggest difference between you and that rich, corporate snob," she said, pulling him down on the couch next to her, "is you *care* about people."

He didn't use to. He never cared for anyone except himself since his parents died, but she had changed that. He cared for her so much it frightened him. He'd also come to care about the ranch and the approval of her uncle. He'd learned to appreciate his own sister. And as for Wayne and the other ranchers? He was growing quite fond of them, too.

Yes, he cared, more than he ever thought possible, and it made what he had to say to her so much harder.

"People like that CEO are just cold-hearted business tycoons who will do anything and use anyone to get what they want without so much as a backward glance," Jenny said, her tone filled with disgust.

"Sell their souls to the devil?" he inquired, lifting a brow.

"Exactly," she said with a grin.

Nick took a deep breath. He didn't like the description. That's not who he wanted to be.

"Jenny, the CEO you heard about on the news does care," he said, taking her hand.

"How do you know?" She looked at him and gasped. "You're from New York, which is close to Boston. Do you know him? Are the two of you related?"

"I *am* the Chandler who attended the Boston charity event, which raised over two million dollars for equine rescue missions."

She looked as if she was about to laugh again, but after studying his face, her expression lost all humor.

"You are . . ." she hesitated, her eyes wide, "rich."

Nick shook his head. "Right now I'm as dirt-poor as you. But the company used to generate a good income."

"When did your finances go bad?"

"Two months ago I found out my accountant embezzled money from the company. I had him brought up on charges but the damage had already been done. Since then the money has dwindled to nothing."

"So until two months ago you were a millionaire?"

"The tabloids stretch the truth. I'm not sure my net worth was quite that high, but—"

"You were a millionaire," Jenny stated, her tone flat.

She tried to pull away from him, her face filled with disgust. He refused to let her go. He wasn't going to let her run, at least not until after he had explained.

"And your reason for the bet? Flirting with me?" Her voice was barely audible.

"When my company's success started to crash I thought I could romance the land away from you."

"And sell it for the money?" She tried to pry loose from his grip. "Sometimes I wish I never owned the land. Everyone always wants the land more than they want *me*."

She tried to turn away. He took hold of her shoulders and turned her back.

"What I never expected was that *you* could romance the land away from *me*," he said, forcing a grin.

"I don't know what you're talking about," she said, taking a solid swing at him with her fist.

He caught the punch with his hand and closed his fingers over hers. "All I want now is *you*. I've never faked how I feel about you."

"How can I be sure?" she demanded.

"Trust your heart," he said, pulling her up against him.

"My heart has failed me in the past, and I have had to live with that mistake and the humiliation of it for six years," she said, twisting out of his embrace.

"Travis never loved you."

"And you do?"

He hesitated and she pushed him aside and began to walk away.

"Jenny, wait—"

"Stay away from me, Chandler," she said, a catch in her voice, and ran from the room.

No. He couldn't lose her. His throat tightened and he gripped the arm of the couch so hard his fingers ached.

What he needed was a plan. *Think.* There had to be

some way of convincing her that his feelings for her were real, but how? He couldn't keep the newspapers away from her forever. If she reacted this badly to the fact he used to be wealthy, what would she say when she found he was the CEO of N.L.C. Industries?

He'd meant to tell her the whole truth, but she hadn't given him a chance. He walked over to the river-rock fireplace and leaned his arm against the top of the stone mantel.

Framed photos of Jenny's family, from generation to generation, stared him in the face. Accused him of trying to disrupt their O'Brien heritage. One person in particular looked at him with more disdain than all the rest.

George O'Brien.

If he were here, what would her father say to him? Would he give permission for him to marry his daughter or tell him to get out of his house?

Turning away from the photographs, Nick feared the latter.

THE CASCADE HERALD delivery truck pulled up beside Sarah's Bakery at five thirty A.M. The lights were on inside the store and the smell of fresh-baked cinnamon buns wafted through the windows. Sarah came out to sign the confirmation clipboard and the delivery man stacked several dozen bundles of newspapers on the front porch.

Nick learned more than he'd ever wanted to know about the Cascade Herald this night. The ten-page local paper was distributed daily to Pine and a handful of neighboring towns.

The articles mostly pertained to cows and crops, and community gossip. But there was one section in the back that regularly reported on the wagers made at the Bets and Burgers Café. Only the most exciting and controversial bets made it to the front page. Jenny had been on the cover the first day he'd arrived in town. Now it was his turn.

An eight-by-ten photo of him wrestling the steer in the rodeo stared back at him in startling black-and-white. If only his options for the future were so clear-cut.

"The delivery man is getting back into his truck," Billie said in a low voice beside him. She'd been his loyal companion since two o'clock in the morning as they drove from town to town in the old ranch truck buying all the local papers before the public got hold of them. "Do you want to go in and talk to Sarah, or have me do it?"

"Talk to Sarah about what?" Nick spun around and locked gazes with the twelve-year-old sitting on a bicycle not three feet behind them. "Josh." Nick stiffened and his mind raced with potential negative consequences the boy's presence could bring.

"You didn't hear me ride up, did you? Like my new bike? It's quiet. Karen Kimball says her dad greased the chain before they sold it to me."

Nick clenched his jaw. "What are you doing here? I thought you only worked weekends."

"I work holidays, too. Today's the Fourth." Josh parked

his bike next to the bakery, and taking out a pocket knife, began to cut the string tying the nearest bundle.

"How would you like the day off?" Nick asked.

"I can't. I have all these newspapers to sell."

Nick stepped closer. "I'd like to help you with that. I'll buy them."

"How many?"

"All of them."

Josh stopped what he was doing and glanced over his shoulder at him, and then at Billie for confirmation. "You're serious?"

Nick nodded and pulled the cash out of his wallet.

"You *are* serious!" Josh exclaimed in the hushed tone of a conspirator. "What do you want to do with them?"

"It's a secret," Nick told him. "I'm going to need you to promise you won't tell anyone who bought them."

"But what do I do if someone asks me why there are no newspapers today?"

"Tell them you sold out."

Josh grinned. "Yes, I did. I really did. Wow! This is going to be the best Fourth of July ever!"

"C'mon, Billie," Nick said, relief soothing his unsettled nerves. "Let's load these into the back of the truck with the others."

"WHEW! THAT WAS close," Billie said, as they unloaded the last of the newspaper bundles at the recycling station. "For a minute, I didn't think Josh would give them to you."

"Neither did I," Nick admitted.

"I guess I better buy another set of alarm clocks to help wake me up if we're going to do this every day."

"We aren't." Nick sat on the tailgate. "This was a one-time deal."

"But you can't let the media tell Jenny who you are," Billie protested. "She'll find out, and when she does—"

"I have one day."

"What do you mean one day?" Billie demanded, hands on her hips.

"Davenport only let me borrow enough money to buy today's papers. I only have one day to tell Jenny who I am and convince her to marry me."

"You can't do it. You need more time," Billie said, her words spilling out in a fevered frenzy. "There must be a way to buy more time. If you tell her who you really are she'll kick us off the ranch. We won't be friends. Wayne and I—Oh Nick, you can't tell her tonight."

Nick shook his head. "I have no choice."

JENNY PICKED HER way across the sun-dried path, trying to avoid the brood of cackling, clucking chickens that crisscrossed in front of her bare, calloused feet. As she shooed them away, another sound met her ears. The sound of a man humming.

Oh, no. She couldn't face Chandler this early in the morning. Mentally bracing herself for her next run-in with her devious, dark-haired ranch manager, she took a deep breath and entered the stable. But when she peeked into the third stall on the right, it was Wayne who turned around to face her, not Nick.

"Why are you so happy?" she demanded.

"Why are you so grumpy?" Wayne countered, and scooped up a pile of shavings with the fork he was using to muck out the floor of the empty stall. "Didn't you sleep?"

"No," she said flatly.

"To be honest," Wayne admitted, "I didn't sleep much either. I haven't been to one of those fancy town dances since my divorce two years ago, but Harry is insisting we all go to this one together. Heck, he's even letting me borrow one of his good shirts. I reckon I better polish my boots as well, don't you think?"

Jenny stiffened. "The Fourth of July dance is tonight?"

"Well, yeah, today *is* the fourth." Wayne looked at her expectantly. "Do you know any girls who might want to dance with me?"

It suddenly occurred to her why Wayne was so happy. He was hoping to dance with her so-called friend, Billie the traitor. Well, it was better he know the truth about the girl before he became too attached, before it hurt too much . . .

Harry came around the corner and she figured it was best he heard it, too.

"The only reason Billie is here is to help Nick win the bet so he can marry me, take my land, and sell it for profit." She looked at Wayne and frowned. "That's why Billie was looking for the gold. The Chandlers seem to have an insatiable quest for fast cash and get-rich schemes."

"Well, you already suspected as much, didn't you?" he asked with a shrug.

"Yes, I did," she admitted.

"Then what's the problem?" Harry asked, coming in and leaning against the door frame.

"I *didn't* know that Nick was a rich playboy millionaire."

Wayne raised his brows and let out a low whistle while Harry chuckled with surprise.

"Gosh, if I'd known he was a millionaire, I would have asked him for more money," Wayne said with a smirk.

She gasped. "You asked him for money?"

"No. We were working in the fields one day shortly after he'd arrived and I mentioned how I was a little short of funds, and well, he was nice enough to offer." Wayne looked down. "I used the money to hire an attorney so I can get the judge to grant me visitation rights with my two little girls."

"Wayne, that's wonderful," she exclaimed, her tone softening. If Wayne was able to see his girls, Sarah would be able to see them, too. The woman hadn't seen her grandchildren in two years and missed them terribly. "How much money did Nick give you?"

"Only a couple thousand. But that's all I needed. I'd saved up the rest."

"See? *That's* the problem. Why was he generous with you? If he cares for me, why won't he give *me* any money?" she said, gritting her teeth. "He knows how desperate I am."

"I think he wants you to marry him first," Harry

grinned. "Gotta hand it to him. He really knows how to get the job done."

"I tried to look Nick up on the Internet. It said Fat Happy Horse Treats is privately owned and I couldn't pull up much information on the company. He also seems to keep his personal life under lock and key. Probably to avoid paparazzi." She shook her head and scowled. "He doesn't need to work. He doesn't need me. He came here for my land."

"But that's not what he'll leave with," Harry predicted. "I knew you two were a match the first time I laid eyes on him."

"What on earth makes you think we could ever be a match?"

"He's as willful and stubborn as you are."

"He only cares about winning," she blurted, trying to hide the ache in her throat. "The bet is a game to him, a way to keep his finances rolling, and I'm just a pawn."

"Aw, that's not all he cares about," said Wayne, pulling her into a hug.

"If you don't mind," said Nick, appearing in the doorway and giving each of the men a direct look before settling his gaze upon her, "I'd like a word alone with Jenny."

"C'mon, Wayne," Harry said, winking at Nick on his way out, "we've got some work to do before we get all dressed up fancy-like tonight."

Wayne gave her a quick reassuring glance before withdrawing his arms. Then he followed Harry out the door. She wished they wouldn't go. She wished they wouldn't leave her alone with him.

The back of her throat ran dry, and her heart raced as he stepped toward her, drawing nearer and nearer, until he was just mere inches away from her face.

"Look at me," he said in a low voice.

"I am looking at you."

"I want you to look into my eyes and tell me what you see."

She fought the urge to squirm under his intense scrutiny. With his body so near to hers it would be impossible to move without brushing against him, and she would rather run into a thicket of nettles than have any kind of physical contact with the man.

"I see a liar," she said boldly.

"What else?"

"A manipulator."

"And?" he prompted.

"A conniving, conceited—"

"What about someone who cares? Do you still see that?"

She hesitated, searching the depths of his eyes for the first time, and was troubled by the stockpile of emotion that lay there waiting for her. Either he was a brilliant actor, or . . .

"Promise you will dance with me tonight, and I'll leave you alone for the rest of the day. Deny me, and I'll stick by your side like a bear attracted to honey."

"I am not honey."

"You're *my* honey," he teased.

"One dance," she said, forcing herself not to smile. "One."

Nick, apparently pleased with himself, grinned and bowed out of her way.

She strode past him on wobbly knees, determined not to convey that he had any effect on her emotions, and got into the ranch truck to make a trip into town.

Her meeting with the bank manager this morning wouldn't be fun, but she would much rather face him than Nick Chandler and his cunning propositions any day.

Chapter Thirteen

"IT'S *PINK*!" BILLIE EXCLAIMED, shriveling her nose in disgust.

Jenny bit her lip to keep herself from laughing as she turned Billie around to face the full-length mirror.

"The dress looks pretty on you, Billie."

"But I don't *wear* pink."

"You will tonight. Here," she said, and handed the young woman a golden tube from off the top of her bedroom dresser. "Put some of this on."

"What is it?"

"Pink lipstick."

"I look stupid," said Billie, folding her arms over her chest. "Everyone's going to laugh at me."

"No one will recognize you." Jenny pinned her friend's caramel-colored hair away from her face. "Not even Wayne."

"He'll tease me to no end."

"I think he'll be speechless."

"Jenny, I can't do this," Billie said, her usual tough-edged voice slipping into an awkward squeak.

"Oh, yes, you can," she said with a devious smile. "You *do* want to help your brother, don't you? Our deal is that if I go to the dance, you have to come along, too. And if you expect me to wear this . . ." she continued, picking up the slinky black strapless designer gown that had arrived from New York earlier that afternoon, "then, *you* are going to wear my old prom gown."

Billie cringed. "Let's just get it over with."

A half hour later, Jenny descended the stairs.

Nick, who had been talking to Harry and Wayne in the kitchen, stared up at her. His gaze slid from her upswept hair to her bare shoulders, and slowly down the smooth, silky length of the black dress, which seemed to mold to her every curve.

Heat rose into her cheeks and her body trembled with self-conscious awareness. Manipulator or not, he could still make her feel like she was someone special.

She tried not to look at him, except she was just as surprised by his appearance as he seemed to be by hers. He was wearing a *suit* . . . and not just any suit, but one of those expensive custom-tailored suits that male models wore on the covers of trendy magazines.

Didn't he know that to most of the cowboys the term "dressed up" usually meant clean jeans and a new flannel shirt? Why, it almost looked as if he was dressed to go to a wedding.

Her stomach flip-flopped crazily to the pit of her

stomach. Surely, that wasn't what he had in mind for this evening.

Her thoughts were abruptly cut off when Billie stepped out from behind her and everyone in the room turned to gape openmouthed.

"What have you done with my sister?" Nick demanded.

"It was Jenny's idea," Billie said, glaring at him. "This is the price I have to pay for being related to you."

Nick grinned, as if he thought the idea of revenge on his sister was funny. Jenny, on the other hand, was more interested in the others' reactions to her transformed friend.

"You look real nice, Billie," said Harry.

"Thanks," Billie stammered, and looked past him at Wayne. "Well, go ahead, just say it. It's obvious from your expression you are just chomping at the bit to mock me."

Wayne shifted his feet and the Adam's apple in his throat bobbed up and down. "You're taller."

Billie's face broke into a big smile, and turning sideways, she lifted the hem of her dress and exposed her four-inch high-heeled shoes.

Wayne gave her a slow grin. "Gee, Billie, you actually look like a girl."

"I *am* a girl, in case you haven't noticed," she retorted. Billie stepped up and punched him in the arm. "Don't you dare laugh at me or I'll kick your butt."

Jenny smiled. Although neither one of them would admit it, she was beginning to think Billie and Wayne would make a perfect . . . match.

An apprehensive shudder stole over her as she remembered Harry using those same words to describe her relationship with Nick. Could it be possible she and Nick, despite his being a hotshot CEO of some million-dollar company, could resolve their differences?

Sure, he was handsome and incredibly fun to flirt with, but a perfect match? The perfect match for a wealthy businessman like Nick Chandler would be the type to have her nails done on a weekly basis and spend her time shopping. She would be elegant and poised, not someone who ate dirt every time she fell off a horse.

Still, she thought, as they filed out of the house and into the waiting trucks, there were times when he looked at her . . . and kissed her . . . that she *wished* she could be his.

THE DANCE WAS already under way when they arrived at the Riverside Pavilion. Jenny took one look at all the men milling about the parking lot and instinctively reached down to adjust the boot knife she'd strapped to her leg beneath her dress.

"Don't tell me you've started wearing weapons again," Nick said, watching her.

"Only for protection."

"When you handed me your knife yesterday, I didn't think you'd get yourself a new one," Nick said, frowning. "I thought it was a gesture you were going to start trusting me."

"I was right not to trust you. I went into town and

found there were no newspapers available today, no papers to feature you or the rodeo. You found a way to keep the editor from printing the story didn't you? Why would you do that, unless you have something to hide?"

"Gol! If you two are going to start bickering, then let me out of the truck." Billie glanced down at the pink ruffles on her dress. "On second thought, why don't *you* get out of the truck and I'll stay."

"We're all going," Jenny said, opening the door.

Maybe she should have stayed home, like Josh's parents. Earlier that day she'd asked Josh if Ed and Shaina were going, and the boy shook his head.

"Doubt it. They'd hate to have to stand that close to each other. They can't stand to be in the same house together. My dad stormed out last night and didn't come home." Josh looked up at her with red-rimmed eyes. "I don't think he's *ever* coming back."

Jenny had assured him his father would, but men and relationships weren't her area of expertise.

As THEY WALKED toward the lighted pavilion next to the river, the band began to play a soft country melody.

"Would you like to dance?" Nick whispered in her ear.

"*Now?*" Jenny glanced at the other couples venturing out on to the dance floor. "We just got here."

"Harry is dancing with Sarah," he said, nodding to her uncle.

"He shouldn't be. He isn't strong enough. He just had heart surgery."

"If you look closer you'll see Sarah's holding him up." Nick held out his hand. "Shall we?"

"Billie and Wayne are headed toward the beer garden, which is where I'd rather be."

"But you don't drink beer," he reminded her.

"Well, then, maybe I'll just enjoy the company," she said, and began to walk away, when Irene's velvety voice stopped her in her tracks.

"I'll dance with you, Nick." Irene smiled up at him with flirtatious eyes and ran her brightly painted red fingertips down the sleeve of his jacket.

"Is it all right if I dance with Irene?" Nick asked, a slow, secretive smile crossing over his lips.

Drat! He knew exactly how she felt about that pretentious, blond-haired tramp and he was deliberately trying to make her jealous.

"Go right ahead," she said, lifting her chin. "It doesn't matter to me who you dance with."

Nick's smile broadened as he took Irene's hand in his and led her to the dance floor.

Walk, she told herself, *and don't look back.* Her feet obeyed, but the vision of Irene in Nick Chandler's arms irked her something fierce. If he really cared about her, how could he dance with that evil wench?

Nick was just playing with her emotions. Was it all a game to him? Is that what rich corporate CEOs did when they were bored? Played games with people? Is that the real reason he had come out here?

She hadn't taken five steps into the beer garden before she was waylaid by David Wilson, Kevin Forester, and

Charlie Pickett. Turning down each of their requests to dance, she was stalled once again by Levi MacGowan's wrinkled knobby hand on her arm.

"What the blazes are you doin' here in that dress without a proper escort?" he demanded, alcohol already heavy upon his breath. He looked at the sleek black gown she was wearing and furrowed his wiry brows. "Would you like me to be your chaperone?"

"Thank you, Levi, but my Uncle Harry is over there," she said, pointing, "and I came with friends who will look out for me."

She sat next to Billie and Wayne at one of the small round wooden tables and stole a quick peek at the couples on the dance floor.

"Irene and Nick look good together, don't they, Jenny?" Billie teased.

She tried to smile, but couldn't. Instead her gaze darted back toward the dance floor and to her horror, her eyes began to sting.

"Would you like to dance with me?" Wayne asked, his voice soft. "If we get close enough to them . . . you can kick her."

"No," she said, shaking her head. "Dance with Billie. She didn't get all dressed up for nothing. I'm going to the bar for some water."

Water seemed like a real good idea at the moment. Her throat was dry and tight. Just as the bartender handed her a filled glass with a slice of lemon, a man in dark jeans and a crisp green rodeo shirt stepped up beside her.

"You look beautiful."

She knew the voice before she turned her head to face him.

Travis Koenig.

"What brings you back to Pine after all these years, Travis?"

"You," he said, flashing a dazzling Hollywood smile. "I missed you."

"And I suppose the town jackpot didn't have anything to do with it?" she countered. "Who told you about the bet?"

"No one. Honest." His tone was sincere, but the twitch of his face confirmed he was lying. "Look, I have a table right back there," he said with a nod. "Could we talk?"

She had every intention of declining, when she caught a glimpse of Nick Chandler staring at her, his expression hard.

"All right," she said, forcing a smile to her face. She followed Travis to a table amid a rowdy crowd of onlookers who gave him the thumbs-up sign as they passed by.

"I know what I did was wrong," Travis began, sitting in the chair beside her and leaning in close, "but I never stopped thinking about you. I never stopped wondering what our lives would be like if I hadn't been such a jerk and hopped into bed with Irene. I came back to say I'm sorry, Jenny, and ask if you have a big enough heart to forgive me."

She nearly choked on the water she was sipping as she listened to him. Travis's words were so practiced, his gestures so smooth, and his manner so self-serving that she wanted to laugh at him. How could she have been so blind as to think she had loved this man, or that he had loved her? Nick was right. Travis had never loved her. The man was only in love with himself.

"I've met someone else," she said, and a strange calm settled within her, "someone who listens when I talk."

"I listen to you," Travis said, draping his arm around her shoulders.

"Someone who cares about what's important to me."

"Now, don't you worry about the ranch. I've got it all figured out. Once we're married and find the gold, money will be rolling in like stones down a hillside."

"Find the gold?" she asked, bristling. "Isn't there anything you care about other than money?"

"I care about you," he said, giving her a wink, "and I won't give up until you agree to be my wife."

"You don't know how to make me feel special," she said in amazement, realizing the truth for the first time.

"Oh, I can make you feel special," Travis exclaimed, and pulling her head forward, he slammed his mouth roughly against hers.

She placed her hands on either side of his head and tried to pry him off, but he was stronger and impervious to her resistance. Panicked, she reached down under the table for her knife. If only she had agreed to dance with Nick . . .

Suddenly Travis's mouth was abruptly ripped off her own and a large fist crashed straight into his face. The blow knocked him backward into the table behind them, spilling the occupant's plate of buffalo wings and mugs of foam-topped beer.

The men and women at the table stood, but instead of being angry, they applauded the unexpected show. In fact, they let out a boisterous cheer when Nick pulled her out of her chair, picked her up by the waist, and hauled her out of the beer garden over his shoulder.

Fireworks had been banned due to lack of rain this season, but from the *ooh*s and *aah*s of the crowd, it sounded like they'd seen their fireworks display after all.

Her last backward glance toward the tables revealed Travis Koenig was still exploding, with curses, oaths, and a colorful bloody nose. She didn't feel sorry for him. His nose would heal a whole lot quicker than his ego.

WHEN THEY WERE clear of the pavilion grounds, Nick continued carrying her over his shoulder straight on through the parking lot.

"Aren't you going to put me down?"

"No."

His tone was stern and discouraged any further argument on her part. Then, just when she thought he might keep her hanging upside down forever, he stopped next to the old ranch truck, opened the door, and put her inside.

Unsure of what was going to happen next, she decided he should be the first one to speak. Except Nick didn't say a word as he slid in behind the wheel and gunned the engine. He didn't even look at her, but kept his eyes focused straight ahead.

Fifteen minutes later he took a sharp turn onto a gravel road, sending dust and rock chips flying. Her hands gripped the seat to maintain her balance and she cast him an agitated glance for his continued silence.

Was he taking her home? No, not home. The truck tore past the usual turnoff and kept going straight. Then, he abruptly steered the truck onto an old logging road, and she caught her breath. He was taking her up to the fire tower on Wild Bear Ridge . . . where they would be utterly alone.

Chapter Fourteen

NICK JERKED THE truck to the left, his knuckles white on the steering wheel. How could she have ever agreed to marry that womanizing jerk? The other men who vied for her affection didn't bother him, but Travis Koenig was someone she had once said yes to.

Torturous visions filled his mind of Travis kissing her, touching her . . .

He pounded his fist on the dashboard, making dust fly up in the air and Jenny cringe in her seat.

If she was going to be with anyone, it was going to be with *him*, and it was going to be *tonight*.

JENNY'S HOPES FOR the evening turned to despair as she twisted the slinky folds of her long black dress around in her fingers. Here she was, dressed in the most elegant gown her body had ever known, and she hadn't even had a chance to dance in it.

No, instead of dancing, she was held captive in the cab of a rickety old pickup by a temperamental madman who was driving like a fiend and refused to acknowledge her existence.

While the trail she'd used for the pack trip wound back and forth around the countryside for hours, the forest service road Nick took went straight up the mountain in thirty minutes.

She stared out the truck windshield wondering if Billie was having a better time than she was, when Nick suddenly gave her a sharp look.

"I can't believe you kissed him."

It wasn't hard for her to figure out who he was referring to.

"I didn't kiss him. Travis kissed *me*."

"Are you still in love with him?"

"Are you jealous?" she countered, and held her breath as she waited for his telling reaction.

"Of course I'm jealous. I'm jealous of anyone who even looks at you."

The growing darkness concealed his expression, but anger shook his voice and his sincerity was clear.

"Good," she said, smiling. "Then maybe in the future you'll think twice about dancing with Irene."

"Did that bother you?" he asked, swerving around a corner and taking the truck up the next steep climb.

"You knew darn well it would bother me," she retorted. "Now you know how it feels."

A deer jumped out of the way as the truck rattled noisily through the dense forest, its headlights finally shining upon the equipment garage at the base of the fire tower. He drove the last few yards and turned off the motor.

"Jenny, if it bothered you that I danced with Irene, then it must mean you care."

"Of course I care," she said, realizing too late where the conversation was headed.

"Then you'll forgive me?"

Perhaps it was the way his head bent toward her with his lips hovering just above her own, or the way the tone of his voice dropped down into a soft caress, but at that particular moment, she was willing to forgive him for . . . almost anything.

"If you meant what you said . . . and you honestly do care for me . . ."

"I do," he said, drawing her closer with his words as well as his arms.

"Then you are forgiven."

She wasn't amazed by the fact he had no trouble finding her lips in the pitch-black darkness. Every time she was near him there seemed to be an invisible rope pulling them together.

Perhaps the legend of Harp Lake was true. Perhaps she and Nick were part of a greater cosmic plan. Perhaps they truly were *meant* to be together.

DREAMS HALF FORGOTTEN rekindled in the back of her mind as he illuminated the fire tower with a flashlight, and led her up the tall flight of creaking stairs.

She no longer cared about missing the dance. The warm air fluttered softly around her, the sky overhead was speckled with an extraordinary array of stars, and Nick was by her side. What more could she possibly want?

She entered the cabin, caught her breath, and froze.

The interior was filled with wildflowers. Daisies, foxglove, lupine, Indian paintbrush. Vases of blossoming color lined every window, flat surface, and shelf on every side of the room and sweetened the air with their natural fragrance.

The table was dressed with a white linen cloth and set with candles, two crystal fluted glasses, and a bottle of wine.

It looked like a scene out of a romance novel.

"So this was all part of a plan?" she asked with amazement and then answered her own question. "Of course it was. You always plan everything."

"I didn't plan on having to kidnap you to get you here," he told her, "but I'm glad I did."

Nick took off his jacket, rolled up the sleeves of his white dress shirt, and turned toward her.

She looked at the shirt and gasped. With his dark locks of hair contrasting with the white . . . she swallowed hard, trying to ignore how devastating his good looks were to her senses. "And what does my kidnapper plan on doing with me now?"

Nick took her hand and led her out onto the open balcony. "You promised me a dance."

"There isn't any music."

"We have all the music we need right here," he replied. "The crickets are chirping, the streams are trickling, and the angels' harps are strumming, down over the hillside. You taught me that."

"Yes, I did," she said, smiling as he drew her into his arms to dance, "but I didn't think someone like you would prefer the sounds of nature to the civilized music of professional symphonies and orchestras."

"*Someone like me?*" he asked, looking down at her, his eyes shining. "You mean someone who *used to have* lots of money?"

She glanced away and he laughed softly as he moved back and forth with her in perfect rhythm.

"I told you I'm broke. But even if I wasn't, I'm still the same person you thought I was, Jenny. Just because I'm the CEO of a large company doesn't mean I'm a rich snob."

"How do I know you aren't pretending? How do I know you aren't trying to win the bet to close a business deal?"

"Trust," he said, looking directly into her eyes. "You have to trust me."

She laid her head against his shoulder. Could she? Trusting anyone was risky and dangerous, but if she trusted Nick, she would also be vulnerable to heartache and pain as well as the humiliation of being duped by a man a second time, if he failed her.

"I won't fail you," he said against her ear.

"Are you reading my thoughts?"

He tightened his arms around her. "There's nothing to be afraid of."

"I met with Davenport this morning. I only had the two thousand to give him out of the twenty I owe on my back debt. The two thousand I made from the pack trip." She gave in to a quick kiss from Nick before she continued. "But while I was in town I ran into a man who might be interested in buying the steers. The whole herd."

Nick's expression lit with excitement. "If he buys the steers, not only will we have the money to save the ranch, but we'll have money to spare to pay off other debts."

Jenny liked the sound of "we." She smiled. "We'll have to find a different way to bring in future income, but we could still grow hay, and I've wanted to turn the ranch into an equestrian center for years. I've never cared much for steers."

"Me neither," Nick said with a grin. "Especially the ones with horns sharp enough to pierce your gut. I'm sure we could make better use of the land."

"I also received a letter from Patrick today," she said, tilting her head back.

"Does he regret selling his property?"

"No. He says he's found a better place."

"And where might that be?"

"In the arms of a woman," she said, and frowned. "He's getting married."

"I've traveled the whole world," he said, freeing the long tresses of her hair from the tight clasp at the back of her head, "and there's no place I'd rather be than right here with you."

Perhaps she was beginning to understand what her cousin had meant. She loved the feel of Nick's arms around her. She loved the exciting sensations he was arousing within her . . .

He drew her close and her whole body responded with anticipation as his mouth—warm, tender, and full of promise—moved teasingly over hers, encouraging her to participate.

She didn't need much coaxing. His playfulness was one of his best qualities, and when combined with his dark hair, handsome face, tanned skin, and the lean muscles that pressed against the thin fabric of the white dress shirt he was wearing, it made him a very difficult man to resist.

Was it just her or was the air growing warmer and more intense? The light breeze had indeed kicked up a notch and whistled as it whipped around them, making the fire tower tremble. The wind didn't bother her, though. She could have withstood a hurricane as long as Nick continued to kiss her like this. Like she was the only woman he'd ever wanted.

He kissed her long and slow until her head began to spin and bells began to ring in her ears. Not bells. She broke her lips away from his. Sirens.

Nick must have heard it, too, for he turned to look out over the fire-tower balcony. Jenny didn't need to move. She could already see the flames from where she stood. She drew in a sharp breath. An orange blaze, chased by the wind, barreled down the mountainside.

"It's headed toward the ranch!" Terror of the worst kind pinched her stomach and squelched all other emotions as she raced toward the stairs..

Her feet didn't seem to be able to move fast enough. If only she could jump or fly, anything to speed her pace. The drum of her boots hitting the wooden planks matched the beat of her heart, each thump a clock-ticking reminder of another moment lost. In her haste, she nearly tripped as she finished descending the first set of steps, but caught herself by grabbing on to the rail. Nick followed on her heels, the beam of his flashlight bouncing crazily off the intersecting structural support posts. Veering around the mid-section platform, they hurried down the second set of steps and finally made it to the ground.

Together they ran for the truck, flung open the doors, and climbed in. Nick shot her an anxious look, then turned the key in the ignition and revved the engine. Thank God it started. Moments later the truck's tires were spinning around turns and bouncing over potholes with even greater speed down the old logging road than it had on the trip up.

Jenny clutched the dashboard so tight she lost feeling in her fingers. She had to remind herself to breathe. To hope. If anything were to happen to the ranch now, she didn't know what she would do.

Chapter Fifteen

THEY HADN'T BEEN driving twenty minutes when they came face-to-face with a wall of fire. Heat filled the truck turning it into an oven. Pine needles sizzled and smoke suffocated the air.

"The road is completely blocked." Jenny glanced nervously from side to side. "We'll have to take the path to the left through the trees."

"Hold on," Nick warned, and stepped on the gas.

The truck went off the road, through the old-growth forest, jostling over broken logs and mossy dips as it made its own path straight down the mountainside.

"My cell phone is in the glove compartment." Nick coughed as they sped through a thick section of smoke. "Try to get ahold of Wayne or Harry."

Jenny found the phone and quickly hit the number.

"There isn't any reception." She shook the phone as if that would somehow help.

Swerving, Nick pulled the truck back on to the old logging road. "It's nearly midnight. Harry has to be home from the dance by now."

Jenny knew he was right. Harry never stayed up late anymore. But what if Wayne took him home and then went back out with Billie? What if her dear old weak-hearted Uncle Harry was at home all alone?

The journey down the mountain seemed to take forever. Nick was driving as fast as he could, but it didn't stop her from wishing she was behind the wheel.

Jenny's great-great-grandfather had named the ranch Windy Meadows because it lay in a valley between Sasquatch Spire and Mount MacGowan. The wind tunneled through like a natural air conditioner to keep them cool in summer, but with the fury of a blowtorch during forest fires.

After snaking around the bottom half of the forest, they finally came out alongside Charlie Pickett's property.

"His back fields are already in flames," Jenny shouted. "It's only a matter of minutes before it reaches—"

She couldn't finish the sentence. Windy Meadows couldn't burn, not after all her efforts to save it. Nick pulled into her driveway and she was out the door and running before the vehicle came to a halt. Wayne's truck was parked next to the house, which meant both Harry and Wayne had made it home. Perhaps if they all worked quickly they could divert the flames.

Nick caught up to her as she ran past the house and together they rushed down the path to the corral where the fire was racing toward them.

Harry wet down the roof of the hay barn with a garden hose and barked directions to Billie and Wayne, who dug a dirt trench around the outlying buildings. Sarah, also there, filled buckets from the outdoor faucet.

Would it be enough? As Nick hurried out to the field to join the others, Jenny ran toward the stable.

A reverberating neigh pierced her ears and was joined by several loud crashes and thuds as she crossed the threshold of the open door. She grabbed a halter and lead rope off the hook on the wall and headed for the first stall where Satan was trying to kick the walls apart.

"Easy, boy," she said, strapping the halter around his big black head and running her hand along the side of his neck. "Let's get you out of here."

Jenny led the frightened horse out the door and with a slap on his rump, sent him running off down the trail to the safety of the open pasture opposite the ranch.

A fire truck arrived, its sirens blaring as it drove past her on its way down to the fields. Kevin jumped out with six of his firefighter friends. Three pickup trucks followed. She paused, and her chest tightened with unexpected gratitude as two dozen fellow ranchers, all carrying shovels and pickaxes, jumped from the backs of the trucks ready to lend a hand.

She hoped her uncle would let someone else take over his position. He wasn't strong enough to be fighting fires.

A plane flew overhead, dropping gallons of water from the air, as she turned to go back through the stable door.

Smoke filled the corridor, and Jenny wished more than ever she hadn't decided to wear the slinky long black gown. It wasn't exactly fire-fighting attire, and it was binding her legs.

Grabbing her boot knife, she ripped through the material, leaving a ragged hemline circling her knees. Next she kicked off her high-heeled shoes, and running barefoot, hurried to Starfire's stall.

The Thoroughbred danced around, almost stepping on her as she unlatched the door. Next she hurried to release Echo and Apache.

"Go on," Jenny urged.

Pushing past her, both horses bolted out the stable entrance.

She rushed to the next stall and jumped backward as a large beam crashed down from the ceiling. Scorching flames shot in all directions, igniting the wooden interior of the building and sending the horses into a frenzied panic.

Time was running out.

Jenny unlatched the sliding locks to every stall door. One horse raced to freedom, while three others, terrified by the sight of the fire, were unable to leave.

Kastle was one of them. The beautiful gray mare reared up and tossed its head, eyes wide.

If only she had a bandanna or a towel to use as a blindfold. Searching the corridor for any scrap of cloth that might work, Jenny spotted the bottom half of her black dress on the ground just twenty feet away.

She was about to retrieve it when an explosion knocked her down amid an avalanche of broken timber. Sparks rained down from the roof. If she could just make it to her feet.

Struggling to free herself from the debris, she glanced up and screamed.

A falling beam was headed straight toward her.

NICK SHIELDED HIS eyes from the searing heat as Kevin Forester pulled him away from the fire line he and the other men were digging.

"Without the wind we'd have a chance," Kevin yelled, "but it's blowing the fire out of control. We have to get out of here while we still can."

Nick nodded. Three air tankers and two helicopters circled above, dropping water and retardant on the flames, but still the fire advanced from every direction.

Another blast shook the ground as the tractor shed exploded and splintering fragments of wood shot skyward.

"My drums of gasoline!" Harry shouted, throwing his arms up into the air.

Spotting Wayne through the smoke a few feet ahead of him, Nick grabbed the back of the ranch hand's shirt.

"Where's Jenny?"

"In the stable," Wayne said, pointing.

The entire structure was engulfed in flames and half of the roof had already collapsed.

"Please, Lord," Nick prayed, taking off on a dead run, "let her be safe."

He entered through the side door and looked down the main corridor but couldn't see her.

"Jenny!" His heart lurched in his chest as he stooped

to pick the bottom half of her dress off the ground. Raising his voice, he called out again. "*Jenny!*"

"Over here."

He followed the sound of her voice and found her inside one of the end stalls.

"My leg is trapped," she said, wincing as she tried to move.

"Don't worry, I've got you."

He pulled off the tangle of beams, but when Jenny tried to stand, her leg gave out beneath her.

"Kastle won't leave her stall," she said, trying to crawl toward the terrified horse. "I have to get her out of here."

"I've got to get *you* out of here first," Nick said, scooping her up in his arms. He was making his way down the aisle when a large figure stepped into the doorway, blocking the exit.

"Frank, what are you doing here?" Jenny exclaimed.

"I told you I'd get you back," the former ranch hand said with a malicious glint in his eyes. "You fired the wrong man, missy. Nice little joke, isn't it? You fired me, and now I am *fire*-ing you."

Nick glanced at the axe gripped tightly in Frank's hands. He wasn't here to help. *He meant to kill them.*

"You set the fire?" Jenny asked, her gaze also on the weapon.

"Of course I did," Frank boasted, raising the axe above his head.

"You won't get away with it," Nick growled.

"Oh, yeah? And who is going to stop me? You? The CEO of N.L.C. Industries?"

Nick gasped, and a ball of dread ripped a hole through his gut, making him feel hollow. Jenny's body went rigid in his arms.

"Oh, yeah, I know your little secret." Frank chuckled, clearly enjoying the moment. "You left one too many bags of cookies lying around the stable. Jenny, did you know Fat Happy Horse Treats are a manufactured product of N.L.C. Industries?"

Nick glanced at Jenny's horrified expression.

"I guess not," Frank said with a grin. "Sorry to spill the beans, Nick."

"The CEO of—" Jenny shook her head. "No, you're wrong. He can't be."

"His full name is Nicholas Lawrence Chandler," Frank informed her. "N.L.C."

Jenny jerked her head around and looked straight into his eyes.

The truth must have been written all over his face, because in the next instant she tried to pull away from him. He continued to hold her tight. "I'll explain later."

"Explain? What is there to explain?"

"I also know about the little scheme you have with my conniving cousin, the bank manager," Frank added.

"What scheme?" Jenny asked, her voice barely audible over the crackling fire.

"Chandler promised Stewart Davenport he'd schmooze the ranch from you and sell it to him." Frank drew back the axe, ready to strike. "Now no one will have it."

The axe swung toward them and Nick leapt to the

side, with Jenny in his arms. Narrow miss. The axe head buried itself in the large wooden support post next to them instead.

A thunderous explosion sounded above and the roof above the beam began to collapse. His heart pounded. Jenny clung to him, her fingernails digging into the back of his neck. He tried to shield her from the raining debris and zigzagged with a series of quick movements to dodge the impending onslaught.

Frank, however, was lit up as bright as the noonday sun. The big man's eyes darted to and fro as the flames raced over his body. But instead of dropping to the ground and rolling, he yelled and ran out the door.

Nick carried Jenny and ran after him, but it was too late. Frank's life was drawn away by the flames right before their eyes.

Two firefighters covered Frank with a blanket and radioed for help as Nick set Jenny on the ground.

"I'll be right back," he promised.

"Where are you going?"

"I've got to get the horses out," Nick said, and turned back toward the stable.

HER MIND NUMB, Jenny sat on the ground staring with disbelief at what was going on around her. The hay barn and equipment shed hovered above the earth like burning specters, with wisps of flame whipping around like fiery arms swatting the firefighters with their anger.

The wretched wails of the cows in the burning field

had diminished. The roar of the fire, cracking of timber, and sporadic whinny from the hillside remained.

She strained to see through the thick mass of dark gray smoke encompassing the horse stable.

Five stables had sat on the ranch before this one. The first had been built for just two horses when her great-great-grandfather laid claim to the land back in 1880. The second was constructed a short while later and lasted forty years. Since then the occasional fire and long-term wear had made it necessary to replace the building again and again. The present stable was going on twenty-five years and could definitely use a few repairs.

Minutes passed. Two more horses ran out the door but still no sign of Nick. She didn't want her horses to die, but she didn't want Nick to die trying to save them either. She was tempted to go after him, but she wouldn't get far with the sprained ankle.

She glanced at Kevin, dressed in his firefighter suit, as he and another fireman carried Frank's charred body away on a stretcher.

"Are you okay?" Billie called, running toward her, "Where's Nick?"

She pointed toward the stable. "He's trying to save the horses."

"The whole thing is an inferno!"

Jenny wrapped her arms around her middle and rocked back and forth, the taste of burnt embers thick on her tongue. Billie was right. The last legs of the stable could collapse at any moment. And the thought of Nick being burned alive like Frank, *like her father*, was more than she could bear.

The sight of the flames transported her back six months before when the old barn had caught fire. Déjà vu disoriented her. Would her father come out? No, her father had died. They'd built a new barn but this wasn't the barn. This was the stable. Would Nick come out? The fire-fighters sprayed a steady stream of water over the top and sides but the building burned brighter and brighter.

Harry walked toward her, a large black smudge on his cheek. "Wayne has the truck running. We have to go *now*."

"My brother is in the stable," Billie squealed, her voice shrill.

Jenny fixed her eyes on the entrance. She waited another thirty seconds . . . forty-five . . . a minute . . . Wayne joined them and asked what was taking so long, why they couldn't leave. Harry placed his hand on her shoulder.

A large gray mass burst through the flames and Jenny jumped to her feet, forgetting her leg was injured. Biting back the stinging pain, she hopped up and down with her weight on one foot and leaned against Billie.

It's him! Jenny could hardly contain herself as Nick's unmistakable outline emerged from the thick smoke. He was running beside Kastle, with her black dress hem over the mare's large gray head.

Billie ran to meet him and he gave his sister a quick squeeze. Then he turned and looked at *her*, his eyes dark with uncertainty, and the present world resumed with amazing focus.

"Nick Chandler is the CEO of N.L.C. Industries," she told Harry and Wayne. "I never knew Nick's middle name. Never put it together. *Nicholas Lawrence Chandler—N.L.C.*"

"*What!*" Wayne demanded. He looked from Nick to Billie.

Harry shut his mouth up tight. What did he think of his choice for a ranch manager now?

Jenny's thoughts turned toward her devious bank manager. Stewart Davenport must have thought he couldn't lose. It was a well-known fact he used his bank position for personal gain. He wanted her property for himself and if he couldn't foreclose on it, he'd have Nick romance the ranch out from under her.

She'd almost fallen for it.

"Jenny, wait," Nick pleaded, grabbing hold of her arm. "Let me explain. Since I met you, all of my original plans have changed." Nick's voice was raw, heartfelt, convincing, until he added, "*Trust me.*"

Trust him? When he'd kept the fact he was the CEO of N.L.C. Industries—the one sending her all the proposals to buy her land—a secret from her? She stared at him and in the back of her mind all she saw was Travis.

"I . . ." She swallowed hard and the horrible suspicion she'd once again been duped by a man who claimed to care about her pushed its way to the center of her thoughts.

"Trust me," Nick repeated in a whisper.

She saw the tension in his face, the desperation in his eyes, but shook her head. "I *can't.*"

Nick's face paled and a muscle jumped along the side

of his jaw. He opened his mouth as if to say something more, but the entire frame of the stable collapsed and the firefighters called for his help. Giving her one last beseeching look, he turned around and left.

A heavy weight filled her lungs, making it hard for her to breathe. Jenny's heart begged to run after him, yet her feet remained glued with firm refusal. She had too many questions, too many suspicions.

Had Nick been faking his emotions the whole time he'd been with her? Her vision blurred as tears forced their way to the surface, spilled over, and ran streaming down her cheeks.

"He cares for you," Billie shouted. "How could you do this to him?"

"How could Jenny do this to him?" Wayne retorted. "And what did he try to do to her? With *your* help?"

"I told him it wouldn't work, that there must be another way, but he wouldn't listen to me."

Wayne scowled. "You knew what he was doing. You could have told Jenny. You could have told *me*. But you didn't. No, instead, you helped your brother every step of the way. At least you and your brother are loyal to each other."

Billie winced as if she'd taken a physical blow, then she ran toward Charlie Pickett's truck, tripping over a hose line in the process.

Jenny doubled over. "Dear God, what have I done?"

"You did what was right," Wayne assured her.

Chapter Sixteen

THE FIREFIGHTERS, ALONG with two dozen able-bodied men, fought the Fourth of July fire in around-the-clock shifts until the blaze was finally contained five days later.

"The rest of it will burn out on its own," Kevin told the small crowd of evacuees gathered in the lobby of the Pine Hotel. "Now we clean up the mess and start over."

Jenny swallowed hard. "I'm not sure if I'll be able to rebuild."

"Instead of rebuilding, some of us might leave," Ed Hanson said, his face drawn.

Ed and Shaina Hanson sat on one of the beige couches, holding hands, with Josh and their other four children sitting on the hardwood floor at their feet. It appeared the fire had brought Josh's parents back together, even if they did have to leave the area.

Jenny glanced at the empty seat beside her. Family and loved ones had come and gone all too swiftly during her life. She'd learned to depend on herself, become self-sufficient. Become strong. She'd always thought strength was a virtue. But the more she looked at Ed and Shaina Hanson, the more she wished she had a hand to hold. As she'd learned when Harry had his heart attack, some tragedies were too hard to go through alone.

She feared losing the ranch would be one of them.

"I've been livin' up in these mountains for darn well near a century," Levi MacGowan said, thumping his cane, "and I don't plan on leavin' now."

"I don't want to leave either," Charlie Pickett said, "but it's not up to us anymore, it's up to Jenny."

"*Me?*" She looked around, trying to read their expressions. "Why me?"

"There's not much sense in rebuilding if we can't access the river," David Wilson said, directing his gaze at her.

Jenny frowned. "I gave permission for each of you to use the easement to the river any time you like."

"Yes, but Stewart Davenport won't," David replied. "If your ranch goes into foreclosure, we'll be forced to sell. Our land is useless without the water access."

"And here I thought you wanted to marry her for the gold," Harry said, joining in. "The real gold isn't *in* the river, it *is* the river, isn't it?"

"My insurance company promised me a check to cover immediate expenses by the end of the week," Charlie Pickett said, "but I'll believe it when I see it. Anyone else heard from their insurance?"

Jenny nodded. "My insurance won't issue a check for at least six weeks. By that time, it will be too late."

A light rain moved in, giving the firefighters the upper hand and extinguishing the last of the danger. Still, Levi MacGowan's place had damage, as well as Charlie Pickett's, the Hanson's, and at least a half dozen others who lived nearby.

"Have you seen it?" Jenny asked, when Wayne returned from the fire line.

"Not yet," he said, shaking his head. "The ranch is still off-limits for another couple of hours."

A couple hours turned into a couple more, but at two o'clock in the afternoon the state patrol allowed Wayne's truck through.

As they drove down the road toward Windy Meadows, Jenny watched the ancient growth of green rolling hills change into an unfamiliar wasteland of nightmarish ash and debris. Charlie Pickett's ranch didn't have a single structure still standing. Her ranch would likely be in the same condition.

Jenny held her breath to stop the tears from spilling, but it only tightened the knot in her stomach.

In time, new trees would grow. The house, barn, stables, fences, and sheds could all be rebuilt. But without the history and cherished memories behind them . . . her ranch would never be the same.

She remembered her mother baking bread and canning jam in the kitchen and how the spicy aroma of apple pie could fill the entire house. She could still see her father sitting in the big easy chair in the living room next to the woodstove, reading the newspaper and smoking his pipe.

How many generations had slid down the old wooden

banister next to the stairs? Or scrawled measurements of their children's growth in the hall closet? She hadn't really thought about it before, but she now realized she'd assumed her own children's measurements would be there someday.

Perhaps she never had a chance to save the ranch despite her best efforts. In any case, the scene over the next hill would tell all.

"Well, splint me together before I fall apart!" Harry exclaimed. "Jenny, are you seeing what I'm seeing?"

"The house is still standing."

"Saved by the finger of God, that's what it is," said Harry. "She's charred on all four sides but somehow still managed to make it through."

Jenny opened the door of the truck as soon as it pulled in the driveway and gasped. It was almost as if an enormous kettle of her uncle's black-bean soup had been poured out over the whole land.

Parts of the charred ground, littered with a variety of melted debris, continued to steam. The hay barn was gone, along with the cow barns and the stable. The remains of the tractor shed lay in a pile of twisted metal.

What really sickened her, though, were the scorched carcasses of her entire herd of Black Angus beef cattle The animals had been out in the pasture, too close to the fire, and unable to escape the fast-spreading flames. She cupped her hand over her mouth and nose. She'd never seen such a wretched sight. Or had to inhale such a ghastly smell. Bile rose in the back of her throat and she turned away.

If only she had sold them sooner. Now she'd have to tell the interested buyer she had no herd to offer him. And in return she wouldn't have the money that could have paid off her entire debt.

Inside the house a different kind of horror awaited her. Although the structure was intact, the interior walls were blackened with soot. Cobwebs that before had hung in the corners unnoticed now eerily stood out in strands of black as if decorated for Halloween. The furniture was covered in a fine film of gray ash and the scent of smoke was embedded in all of the rugs and curtains.

Every item in the house needed to be washed before any of them could move back in. *If* they were going to move back in. She, Harry, and Wayne had spent the last week at the Pine Hotel and her financial deadline was only three days away.

"I don't know what to do," Jenny confessed.

"You can still ride." Harry handed her a copy of the *Cascade Herald*.

She read aloud, "The annual Pine Tree Dash, which had been canceled last Saturday due to wildfire, has been rescheduled for this coming Saturday, July thirteenth."

Harry nodded. "Thirteen may be your lucky number after all."

Jenny laid the newspaper on the kitchen table. "How could the outcome of so many things hinge on a single day? The bet ends on the thirteenth, so for spite the bank manager moved up my foreclosure deadline to the thirteenth, and now the race is on the thirteenth, too?"

"No one could have predicted the fire or that it would cause the race to be rescheduled for the following week," Harry told her. "You know the saying, Events tend to happen in threes?"

She smiled. "I've also heard that when it rains, it pours."

"How about, there's no such thing as coincidence?" her uncle challenged. "Or, everything happens for a reason?"

"You win," Jenny said. "I'll sign Kastle up for the race—just as soon as I find her."

Jenny went back outside and called for her horses. At first there was no response, then in the distance there were a couple of answering neighs. Twenty minutes later, Starfire trotted up the driveway.

His face and parts of his bay coat were smudged black with charcoal and ash, but he didn't have any burns on his body. Jenny threw her arms around him and the Thoroughbred nuzzled her hair.

"Hey, big boy. I'll need you to help me round up the others."

Slipping a handmade rope halter over Starfire's head, she hopped on the horse and rode him bareback up the forested trail. Just as she hoped, Starfire began to nicker to his lost stable mates.

The first one they found was Kastle. Jenny slid out of the saddle and noticed the mare was favoring her right hind leg.

"Easy, girl."

Jenny ran her hands down along the fetlock and felt some swelling. The skin was hot. When she lifted the hoof, Kastle flinched and her worst fears were confirmed.

Kastle, the horse she'd wanted to ride in the Pine Tree Dash, was lame.

NICK FINISHED HELPING Kevin wrap the fire hoses for the night and headed toward the Bets and Burgers Café. Pete Johnson and his daughter Irene had been nice enough to give him and Billie a place to stay. But for how long? Sooner or later, he'd have to face the fact he needed to book a flight back to New York.

He didn't want to leave Jenny behind. Somehow over the last few weeks the bet he'd made with her had become real. Only he didn't just want to marry her. He wanted her love.

Before she'd learned he was the CEO of N.L.C. Industries Jenny *acted* like she was in love with him. But he'd been misled by women's body language before. He wasn't going to be fool enough to believe it until she said the words. So far, she hadn't, and at this point he doubted she ever would.

Billie brought him a hamburger and sat beside him on the café steps. Dark rings circled her eyes, and she appeared smaller, more frail than he'd ever seen her.

"I'm so sorry, Nick. So sorry."

"I know."

They sat in silence, each in their own misery. Billie hadn't mentioned Wayne's name, but she didn't have to. Nick knew his sister had taken a secret liking to the sandy-haired ranch hand as much as he had come to care about Jenny. And now they'd lost them, along with any chance of paying off Billie's debt.

Never had he felt so powerless.

Later, when he was alone, Nick sat on the edge of his borrowed bed mattress and dropped his head into his hands. He'd flown to Pine to deceive Jenny, and he'd succeeded. He just hadn't realized how much his actions would cost him. He'd been so focused on money to save his sister he'd become disoriented. Lost his values. Lost Jenny.

You don't deserve her. The accusing words tumbled about in his mind, and condemned him. He didn't deserve her. He would never deserve her. She was better off without him.

But it would be hell on earth to have to let her go.

"God help me," he pleaded aloud, and found himself on his knees without any conscious recollection of having slid down to them.

SARAH HELPED JENNY scrub the house to remove the gray film the fire had left behind. Perfume and floral candles helped to re-scent the air. And the washing machine became their most prized appliance. Everything in the house needed to be assessed for damage.

Jenny opened the cedar chest in her parents' old bedroom and found her mother's wedding dress. The dress she'd hoped to be married in someday.

"Does it smell like smoke?" Sarah asked.

Sarah Gardner had been her mother's best friend—until cancer separated them.

"No," she said, running a finger along the low-necked antique white gown with cap sleeves. She hugged it to her body, held out the long train with multiple inset lace designs, and looked at herself in the mirror. Would she ever marry?

She kneeled next to the chest to search for her mother's jewelry and pulled out an old envelope.

"It's a letter from my great-great-grandfather to my great-great grandmother."

She removed the fragile page and read:

My dearest Katherine, the new boys pan the river for gold with a zeal that disheartens my soul. Greed has taken hold of their hearts so they do not recognize true wealth. I told them I found more gold than they'd ever seen, indeed, a gold mine. I long for you to re-join me here in Pine so they can see firsthand the value of relationships. You are my most precious treasure, my own pure gold, and your love has made me a rich man.

> *Forever yours,*
> *Shamus*

Sarah sighed. "Wow."

"*She* was the gold," Jenny said, and sat back on her heels. "The gold mine he found was my *great-great grandmother.*"

"The men at the café will be disappointed," Sarah predicted. "They hoped the old journal entry would lead to another gold rush."

"Me too." Jenny's shoulders slumped. "It would have been nice to find a big gold nugget in my yard. I could have saved the ranch. Now I have nothing."

THE HOT RAYS of midday sun streamed through the bedroom window. Jenny pulled the sheet higher to block the intrusive light. If only she could block the memories.

Memories of how Nick's intense gaze could make her feel self-conscious, exhilarated, and beautiful all at the same time.

Memories of his deep, smooth voice calling her name. His amused laugh. His playful grin.

Memories of his warm embrace. His lips against hers. His passionate, heart-swaying kiss.

She wore his navy blue T-shirt, a foolish gesture, but she didn't care. The clean smell of the sandalwood soap he used clung to the weave.

He hadn't called. Hadn't tried to contact her. Hadn't come back to collect his and Billie's personal possessions. Not even his precious laptop.

Was he thinking of her? Would she ever see him again?

She missed him. She'd been manipulated and deceived by a man who sought nothing more from her except her land, and yet . . . she still missed him.

How pathetic was that? She dissolved into a renewed

bash of tears as she rolled into a ball and hugged her knees against her chest.

There wouldn't be any more teasing banter across the dinner table, or anyone to make her heart dance as she mucked the horses' stalls, or any children with dark hair and mischievous silver-gray eyes running around the ranch.

She must be the stupidest girl on the planet to have believed Nick cared for her. Heck, she'd even daydreamed he was in *love* with her. And she with him.

Love.

A sharp ache tore through her heart. Filled her with despair. Tormented her soul. Was there no one out there in the world for her? Would she live the rest of her life alone?

She didn't like wallowing in self-pity any more than a knee-high pile of manure. Better to keep moving. Chores needed to be done—at least for one more day—and she didn't want to give Harry an excuse to start working again.

Jenny climbed out of bed, dressed in her barn clothes and descended the stairs. She was halfway across the kitchen when the sound of shattering glass drew her attention. She changed direction and hurried into the living room.

"Wayne? Are you all right?"

His unshaven face hovered over the bar, the broken stem of a crystal goblet in his right hand and a bottle of scotch in his other.

"Sorry about the mess," Wayne said, his sullen expression instantly contrite.

"I'll clean up." Jenny bent to pick up the pieces and waved him off toward the door.

Wayne hesitated, and then sauntered away, taking the bottle of scotch with him.

Poor Wayne. Billie's absence had the same effect on him as Nick's absence had on her.

She stared at the broken glass stretched across the carpet, each shard a glistening reminder that it had once been part of something beautiful.

JENNY PULLED THE blue tarp off the hay bales, loaded the wheelbarrow, and headed toward the makeshift corrals. The horses pawed the ground and snorted as she approached, anxious to get their food.

"Sorry, I'm late," she said, and tossed them each a flake of alfalfa. "I know how impatient—"

Jenny did a double take. Kastle pranced with the others . . . without favoring the injured leg.

She slipped inside the pen and unwrapped the bandage around the mare's hock. No swelling. Perhaps the herbs she'd put on the wrap had speeded the recovery. Could the horse be healed?

Jenny finished feeding the other horses. Then she rode Kastle bareback down to the river to see how much pressure the mare could handle. Kastle was restless. The horse pulled at the reins and wanted to fly. The rhythm of hooves increased the rhythm of Jenny's heart, and her thoughts headed straight toward the Pine Tree Dash. Was Kastle up for it?

If the mare showed any sign of weakness, she'd drop out of the race. She'd never cripple an animal to save her ranch. But if she won? Could she get the prize money to the bank manager in time?

Her father once told her she was only a failure if she stopped trying—and, by golly, she wasn't going to give up now. Her ancestors were fighters, and so was she.

"C'mon, girl," Jenny said, and turned Kastle back toward the ranch. "We have a race to win."

Chapter Seventeen

JENNY LOADED STARFIRE'S tack into the horse trailer the following morning, her mind bursting with renewed hope.

"Got company," Wayne warned.

She expected to see Sarah. Harry had said she'd planned to visit.

But it was that devil, Irene Johnson, who walked straight toward her. Except her blond curls lacked their usual bounce, and instead of high heels, the woman had actually donned a pair of brown loafers.

What the heck was *she* doing here?

In all the years Jenny had known her, Irene had never stepped foot on the ranch. Jenny turned from the trailer to face her. Both Harry and Wayne drew near.

"Hi, Jenny."

Jenny tried to think of something civil to say. Nothing came to mind.

Irene held up her hand. "Look. I know what you think of me, but I thought you should know the truth."

Jenny crossed her arms over her chest. "What truth?"

"Billie owes a lot of money to an Atlantic City casino owner and Nick couldn't pull cash out of N.L.C. Industries to help her. The three parcels he owns in Pine were originally purchased to build a new shipping center. Nick thought he could sell them to get the money, but only one buyer was interested."

"Stewart Davenport," Jenny stated, her voice dry.

"It was Davenport who put the idea in Nick's head to try to woo the land from you. He said he wouldn't buy Nick's land unless yours was included in the deal. Don't you see? Nick was just trying to get the money to protect his sister."

"It doesn't excuse what he did to *me*," Jenny said.

"He may have come with wrong intentions, but he didn't actually *do* anything to hurt you, did he? You just assumed he would. He asked you to trust him and you refused." Irene sighed. "Nick isn't asking for his original *intentions* to be excused. Maybe all he hopes for is a little understanding and forgiveness."

Irene gave her a hard look before she walked away, and Jenny bit her lip. She hated the way Irene made her feel.

Like *she* was the bad guy.

THE SMELL OF fresh-baked garlic and Parmesan-cheese bread wafted from the bakery when Jenny, Wayne, and

Harry arrived in the old extended-cab pickup to offer Sarah a ride to the race.

"I don't think I can go," Sarah said.

Harry frowned. "Why not?"

"I think someone needs to keep an eye on Billie," Sarah told them, her soft face creasing. "She hasn't slept in three days and has been roving around town like a zombie. I don't think she really meant to hurt you, Jenny. I don't think either of them did. Nick looks just as bad. I saw him this morning but it didn't seem like he was really there, if you know what I mean."

Jenny didn't want to cave in to feeling sorry for them, to believe they cared, but her chest tightened anyway.

"Where are they now?" Jenny asked.

"Billie is behind the bakery."

"She's here?"

Jenny thought of the connection she'd felt the day Billie had burned dinner, the sympathetic look the tomboy had given her when she'd taken her mother's ring to the pawn shop. The fun they'd had digging for gold. Fun dressing in their gowns for the dance. Her throat closed and she turned to give the others an apologetic look.

"I'm sorry. I may be an idiot, but . . . I have to go to her."

Wayne's face lit into a slow grin. "So do I."

Jenny rounded the back corner of the bakery and found Billie on the ground, propped against a giant old-fashioned wooden water barrel with her eyes closed.

"C'mon, wake up." She gave each of her friend's cheeks a light slap.

Wayne shook Billie's shoulder.

Jenny poked her in the ribs and exchanged a quick glance with Wayne. "She isn't responding. Sarah said she hadn't slept in three days and when Billie *does* sleep she's impossible to wake up. What are we going to do?"

"Get wet."

A crooked grin broke out across Wayne's face and lit his eyes as he gazed down at Billie with a look of tender adoration. Then he scooped Billie into his arms and threw her feet first into the water barrel.

The spray flew into the air and rained cold droplets over their heads. A wave spilled over the barrel's rim. Then the surface of the water bubbled, a head popped out, and obscenities assaulted their ears.

Billie shook like a wet dog and barked angrier than a pit bull defending its prized bone. "How dare you—"

Placing his hand on top of her head, Wayne dunked her under again.

The second time she came up, she gasped for air and took a swing at him. She missed, and Wayne took the liberty of dunking her a third time.

When Billie broke the surface her face contorted and her gasps turned to giant sobs.

"What do you want from me?"

"The race starts in an hour," Jenny said in a rush. "And I want . . . I *need* you there by my side."

"I thought you said you didn't trust us."

"I'm so sorry I ever doubted you, Billie. Please forgive me. I should have allowed you and Nick to explain."

"I'm sorry I yelled at you," Wayne added. "I guess we all jumped to conclusions."

"I suppose I jumped to conclusions, too." Billie locked eyes with Wayne. "I guess I was wrong to think you had any interest in me. I must've been a total moron, a fool, a stupid clod, to follow you around like some lovesick—"

Jenny gasped as Wayne reached out with both hands, grabbed her soggy-haired friend by the shoulders, and *kissed* her.

"I *am* interested, Billie," Wayne said, pulling back. "I didn't want to be, but I am."

Billie's cheeks flushed crimson, and she shifted her gaze to Jenny. "Didn't you say we have a race to get to?"

Jenny nodded.

"Then why are we still standing here?" Billie demanded.

Jenny smiled, glad to have her friend back. She only wished Nick was with them.

JENNY PARKED THE ranch truck in Levi MacGowan's charred mountainside field and gazed across Harp Lake to the camp under the fire tower where she and Nick had first kissed. She wished she could hear the harps again and be reassured they were meant to be together, but she had a race to win. She needed to remain focused. Fifty other trucks and horse trailers lined the lot and promised a tougher competition than any other year.

Kastle was young and didn't travel well by herself,

so they'd brought Starfire along, hoping the older horse would calm her down. It worked. Both horses basked in the sun with their eyes half closed, oblivious to the whirl of people who walked back and forth beside them.

"The Pine Tree Dash is open to both English- and western-style riders," Jenny explained to Billie. "There are only two rules—stay on the trail, and no endangering the horses or other competitors."

"It's not a regulated event," Wayne added. "Just a bunch of cowboys racing on a privately owned back-country trail. Each competitor puts in two hundred dollars and the first one across the finish line gets the money."

"Is that legal?" Billie asked.

"It's tradition," Levi MacGowan said as he joined them. "The Pine Tree Dash dates back to the early nineteen hundreds, when my ancestors decided this old town needed to offer hope to those who hadn't found any gold. We'll be usin' the Winding River Trail, which runs through my property and finishes back here at Harp Lake."

He turned to Jenny. "The blasted reporters think you're their top news story since the *Cascade Herald* publicized your bet with the CEO of N.L.C. Industries. They're askin' my permission to film the race. At first, I told 'em to git off my land. But when they offered to dump a pile of money into the winner's pot, I said I'd have to ask you first."

"How much money are we talking about?"

Levi's mouth curved into a grin beneath his white woolly moustache. "Five thousand each crew, and there's about twenty of them."

"One hundred thousand dollars," she exclaimed, "on top of the ten thousand put up by the competitors."

"Enough to save your ranch, maybe this whole town."

"Then tell them to come."

"That's my girl," Levi crowed. "I'll have everyone we know bettin' on you."

"No pressure or anything," Billie added with a grin.

Jenny cringed. She wasn't fond of reporters or bets, but a hundred-and-ten-thousand-dollar prize would not only pay off her bank loan—it could also pay for a new stable and allow her to offer assistance to her neighbors.

Maybe Alan Simms, the pesky *Cascade Herald* reporter she'd dubbed the rat-man, wasn't so bad after all. She might even have to thank him.

If she won.

While Harry and Sarah waited in line to sign her in, Wayne and Billie went off to have a private conversation, and promised to meet her at the finish line.

Jenny checked Kastle's leg. Still no sign of weakness. Then she called Nick's cell phone. Still no answer.

"Well, if it isn't the most popular bachelorette in town," a voice purred close to her ear. "Will you marry me, Jenny?"

She leapt aside, and turning, stared into the face of Travis Koenig—her former fiancé—who stood next to the county sheriff. "What do you want?"

"I've come to collect this horse," he said, and took hold of Kastle's halter.

"This is *my* horse. Get your hands off her."

"She's Stewart Davenport's horse now," Travis said.

"I'm afraid he has the certificate of ownership," the sheriff informed her.

"How did you get that?" she asked, staring at the paper Travis held up with Nick's signature on it.

"Chandler used the ownership papers as collateral for a small loan Davenport gave him. Since the fire took his salary, Chandler hasn't been able to pay the loan back as promised, so the horse no longer belongs to him."

Jenny couldn't move. Couldn't breathe. She'd meant to ask Nick for Kastle's paperwork after the auction but forgot.

"You can't do this," she said, her throat raw. "I need her for the race."

"No," Travis smiled. "*I* need her for the race."

"You're racing for *Davenport*?"

"Anything for the money, honey."

Jenny scowled. "You did me a favor when you didn't show up at the church."

"I did *myself* a favor," Travis said, with a sneer. "I could never be tied to just one woman."

Jenny clenched her teeth as he led Kastle away, and wished she'd never laid eyes on him.

Uncle Harry returned to the horse trailer with her competition number a few minutes later. "Where the heck is Kastle? And why are you sitting on the ground?"

"Travis took her," she said, lifting her tear-streaked face from the crook of her arm. "Davenport has Kastle's ownership papers and plans to have Travis ride her in the race."

Harry bellowed at the top of his lungs and a group of

ranchers hurried forward to see what was wrong. In between ranting and raving her uncle managed to fill them in.

"You could ride Blue Devil," Kevin Forester offered.

Jenny shook her head. "Kastle beat Blue Devil in a race the week before I bought her."

"She can't give up." David Wilson turned toward the other ranchers. "If she doesn't win the race, we'll all be a bunch of homeless beggars sleeping on the streets."

"I've seen her practice," Uncle Harry told them, "and I can tell you there's not another horse faster than that gray mare in Okanogan County."

"There is *one*," Jenny said, as she stood up and brushed herself off. "I could ride Starfire."

"You got Kastle because you thought Starfire was too old," Uncle Harry reminded her.

"Starfire may be old, but he's won the Pine Tree Dash three times."

"He hasn't raced in over four years."

"He races at home." Jenny carried Kastle's western saddle back into the trailer and returned with Starfire's English riding gear. "I know it's a long shot. I also know the strengths and weaknesses of both horses."

NICK SPRANG FROM the truck and scanned the maze of people, horses, and parked trailers to search for Jenny. He spotted her toward the far side of the field, lined up to ride on Starfire. Where was Kastle?

Realizing Davenport must have taken the mare, he

groaned. Jenny's fury toward him had probably doubled, but he had to speak to her.

He cut through the crowd as fast as he could, pushing some people out of the way, and weaving around others. But he was afraid he wasn't going to make it in time.

"Jenny!"

She turned her head and looked right at him, but a second later the starting whistle blew and the riders took off.

He was too late.

He watched her disappear into the trees, and wondered how long the race would last. How long before he could talk to her . . . and say good-bye.

"There you are, Chandler. I've been looking for you."

He recognized the voice behind him and froze. He'd known this day would come but he still wasn't ready for it.

Slowly he turned around and there in front of him stood Victor Lucarelli and six of his men.

JENNY KEPT STARFIRE at a canter as they rounded the first sharp corner of the trail. A fence bordered the right-hand side of the path and a burnt hedge bordered the left. They couldn't pass the riders in front of them. They had to wait.

Then the hedge came to an end and the fifty riders entered in the race began to spread out. A space opened; Jenny took it, and urged Starfire forward.

A few minutes later they moved into the front half of the group, but her mind wandered back to Nick.

Her heart had nearly leapt out of her chest when he'd called to her. After not seeing him for an entire week, he'd come. And called out her name. If the start whistle hadn't blown when it did, what would he have said to her? Would he be there, waiting for her, when the race was over?

It's true he hadn't been truthful with her about his identity. His intentions hadn't been honorable. But he'd worked hard to help the ranch succeed. He'd saved her Uncle Harry's life, her life, and the lives of her horses. If he cared for her, didn't he deserve a second chance?

If only she could be certain he *did* care.

Amid the thunder of hooves the sharp crack of a whip rang in her ears and Travis Koenig drove Kastle straight in front of her. Starfire veered. If she hadn't kept a firm grip on the reins, the thoroughbred could have slipped off the steep embankment.

She readjusted her seat, and would have called Travis several of the names she'd heard Billie use, except he was already too far ahead to hear.

"Go after him, Jenny." Kevin Forester rode Blue Devil up on her left. "You can do it. Take the bull by the horns."

Easy to say, harder to do.

As the elevation increased, so did the number of sharp turns up the craggy hillside. The switchbacks made it difficult once again for anyone to pass, and to her dismay, Travis remained more than six riders ahead.

A rumble sounded above and she glanced at the cliff on her left.

"Rockslide," someone shouted.

Jenny's adrenaline shot into high gear as she and Starfire raced to avoid the onslaught of stones tumbling down the mountain. The ground was loose from the forest fire. Without the trees and bushes to hold the rocks in place, the slightest disturbance could initiate a slide. For one fateful second she cringed and thought they'd roll to their death. Then the roar of the avalanche fell away from her and echoed across the valley below.

"That was close," Kevin yelled from behind.

It was indeed. She looked back over her shoulder and drew in a sharp breath.

Four feet of debris blocked the path and brought the race to a premature end for half the riders entered.

To win, she needed to reach the band of riders in front of her who vied for first place.

The trail widened and the trees parted to reveal an open field. Jenny loosened the reins and leaned forward in the saddle. Starfire gave a shrill whinny and picked up his pace from a canter to a full run.

They passed three riders, a fourth, a fifth. Travis, racing against her on her own horse, was fifty yards ahead.

Nick, too, had always been one step ahead. He'd challenged her, drawn her out of her self-imposed hermit status, and reintroduced her to the world again.

She'd told Wayne that Nick and Billie were on an insatiable quest for fast cash, but then again, wasn't *she*?

Isn't that the reason she accepted the bet with Nick? To get some "easy money"? Maybe if she'd stopped thinking about the money for one moment, stopped being so materialistic . . . but wasn't it right to want to keep one's home?

What if she lost the race? Lost the ranch? Where would she go? What would she do? Would she meander down to California and try surfing with her cousin Patrick? What about Uncle Harry? Her thoughts swirled so fast she couldn't think straight. Good thing her horse knew what to do.

Starfire jumped over a fallen log, raced around a fire-damaged bridge, and splashed straight through a network of shallow streams. They passed more riders whose mounts had begun to tire. She lost sight of Travis when they rounded the curve, but he and Kastle had to be close.

She'd been on this trail dozens of times with Levi and her father when they hunted elk. A half mile remained and she couldn't waste a single second. Every moment, every step, from this point on, mattered.

And yet, she continued to think of Nick, his silver-gray eyes upon her, his expression earnest, as he asked her to trust him.

Her need to see him intensified her need to cross the finish line. Jenny squeezed her legs and pushed Starfire past two more riders. Both Kastle and the finish line beside Harp Lake came into view at the same time.

Starfire was exhausted. She could feel the tension in his muscles. He wouldn't be able to last much longer.

"C'mon, boy," she whispered. "You can do it."

Starfire gained speed and caught up with the gray mare. The noise of the horse's hooves drummed in Jenny's ears and chest.

The terrain dipped and when they crested the next hill, Jenny saw the large fallen tree sticking out across one side of the path. Blackened trunk. No branches. Two and a half feet high. No problem for her to jump. Starfire rode English.

What would Travis do? A jump in a western saddle would hurt, the horn would gouge his stomach, but it *could* be done.

Jenny glanced with concern at Kastle's legs. The mare's prior injury remained unnoticed, but it could still be tender. Too tender to attempt a jump. If she could get Travis to follow her, Kastle might refuse to go over the log and allow her and Starfire to win.

When Travis glanced at her she gave him a sweet smile and steered Starfire toward the left making it clear she intended to jump. Just like she hoped, Travis gave her a smug look and did the same. His ego would never allow him to let her have the upper hand. He planned to beat her and win with style.

He was also smart. He knew riding around the tree would cost precious seconds. Time he didn't have with her and Starfire riding beside him.

Kastle tried to pull the reins out of Travis's hands, but the former rodeo star held on and refused to relinquish control. He smacked his crop against the mare's hind quarters.

"Travis, no! Don't force her!"

Travis ignored the protest and headed straight toward the log.

Faster. Faster. Starfire snorted, his eye on Kastle as the gray mare widened the distance between them by several feet.

The fallen tree drew closer. Travis crouched over the mare's neck.

Jenny held her breath, dread already rushing into the pit of her stomach as Kastle's muscles flexed.

Drat! She'd been right. Kastle *was* the horse to win the race. After Travis and Kastle made it over the jump, there would be no way to catch up with them. They'd already be too far ahead.

Then Kastle pulled up short at the last second. Pitched Travis sideways. Starfire's muscles bunched and a second later she and Starfire soared into the sky. Sun kissed the top of her head. Wind blew back her hair. They rose higher and higher as if lifted by a giant hand. Jenny laughed. Giddy. She was *free*.

Incredibly, deliriously, unbelievably free!

The bank would never be able to take her land away from her now. The horses, the house, the fields, everything she loved that hung in the balance of this jump would finally be free of outside threat.

Tears filtered down her face as Starfire's hooves met the ground. Harp Lake beckoned like a beautiful unspeakable mirage. Loud cheers and spontaneous applause greeted them as they crossed the finish line.

They did it. They won.

Jenny wiped her face with her hands, broke into a

smile, and wrapped her arms around her beloved horse.

"That's my good boy," she whispered.

Starfire's ears twitched at the sound of her voice, and he whinnied his acceptance of the praise.

Jenny walked him in circles to give him a chance to catch his breath and the frenzied photographers an opportunity to take a picture. The other riders continued to come in. Several of them nodded to her. Kevin saluted. Travis eyed her with contempt.

She'd never know why Kastle refused the jump. Maybe the mare's leg was still tender. Maybe the horse remembered the accident that gave her the scar or didn't have much experience. Or maybe Kastle just didn't like Travis.

No matter the cause, Davenport's abrupt acquisition of her horse prior to the race had worked to her advantage.

Harry chuckled and gave the thoroughbred an affectionate pat. "See? Old age doesn't mean you're out of the race. I think we both have a bit more life in us."

Billie ran forward. "Wow! That was great. We saw you win from the top of the hill."

Wayne lagged behind, his walk slow and his face pale.

"What's wrong with him?" Jenny asked.

"I don't know." Billie frowned. "He's been like that ever since we passed the lake."

"Did you say anything to him?"

"I told him I heard harps."

"Harps?" Jenny slid out of the saddle and grinned. "Give him time. He'll get over it." She paused, afraid to ask. "And Nick?"

Billie shook her head. "I haven't talked to him."

Levi, David, and several others also came to offer their congratulations.

"I knew you could do it, girl." Levi's old wrinkled face beamed as he handed her a bag filled with money. "You might need an escort to keep you safe with all that cash."

"The bank closes in a half hour," said Harry. He took Starfire's reins. "You have to hurry."

Jenny glanced from her truck at the far end of the parking lot to David Wilson's, fifteen feet away.

"David, can you give me a ride?"

The rancher whipped his keys out of his pocket. "You bet I can."

Chapter Eighteen

DAVID WILSON SHOULD have been arrested for the way he sped into town. The truck shot around turns, spit gravel, and squealed louder than a wayward missile.

Jenny braced one hand on the dashboard while the other gripped the edge of her seat. She didn't know whether to be scared or thankful, but her need to get to the bank had her leaning toward thankful.

The clock above the building read 12:20. Jenny looked through the large bay window as David squealed to a stop, and saw the financial manager still at his desk.

She'd made it just in time.

The bank closed 12:30 on Saturdays. A fact she'd forgotten when Stewart Davenport bumped up her deadline to this date. The bet didn't end until 1:00 and if the prize money from the race wasn't raised, she wouldn't have been able to save her ranch.

She and David hopped out of the front of the truck, while Wayne, Billie, Kevin, and Levi, who hadn't wanted to be left behind, climbed out of the back.

Jenny hurried to the bank entrance.

"Jenny, wait!"

She hesitated. Turned around. "Josh?"

The twelve-year-old ran toward her. "Nick's in a fight! Seven men pulled him out of a big black limo and one of them punched him in the stomach. Pete Johnson called the sheriff but by the time he gets here it will be too late! They are really big. I've never seen such big men. Bigger than Ted Andrews!"

Billie fell to the ground on her knees, her eyes wide. "They're going to kill him! *Oh, no! No! No! No!* What should I do? I can't go over there. If I go over there they will kill me, too!"

Wayne put a hand on Billie's shoulder. "I won't let anyone harm you."

"You don't understand. I owe Lucarelli a hundred grand. It's all my fault. Everything that's happened is all my fault. I never should have gambled, never should have cheated. Now the guy I owe is *here* with his men and they're going to make Nick pay."

"I won't let him stand alone," Wayne said, his voice firm. "Where are they?"

Josh pointed down the street. "Behind the Bets and Burgers Café."

Wayne ran off and Jenny moved to go after him, when David placed a hand on her arm. "What are you doing?"

The ranchers stood stock-still and tombstone quiet as

they waited for her reply. Even the breeze died down as if it, too, wanted to listen.

Jenny glanced down at the bag in her hand, more money than she'd ever held in her entire life, and her stomach twisted in knots.

"I—I can't let them hurt him." She eyed each of the ranchers as if daring them to protest. "Could you?"

The ranchers hesitated, and then slowly shook their heads, their expressions grim. Levi pulled at his whiskers. David scuffed the dirt with the toe of his boot. Jenny looked at Billie and a multitude of sad unspoken words conversed between them.

Turning, Jenny hurried toward the café.

When she rounded the corner she saw them. Seven men, dressed in various shades of black and blue, one of them grasping the front of Nick's shirt.

"*Stop!*" she shouted. "I have the money Billie owes you."

The men all looked at her with surprise, including Nick, as she stepped forward and placed the bag of money into the nearest man's hands.

The man glanced around at his comrades, turned back to her, and smiled. "Thank you, but the debt has already been paid."

"It has?" Jenny gasped as he handed the money bag back to her. "How?"

The man holding Nick by the front of his shirt released him and Nick brushed himself off. "I gave him N.L.C. Industries."

She saw the heartbreak in Nick's eyes. Knew how

much the company meant to him and how much it hurt to let it go. She glanced at the first man who had spoken, the one who seemed to be in charge.

"Then what is all this about? Why did you bruise Nick's face if he already paid you?"

The lead man grinned. "This is for the interest."

"Well, are you about finished?" she demanded, raising her own fist toward him.

The seven men looked at her and laughed.

"I think we are," the lead man said, and the other men began to step away.

Wayne hurried to Nick's side and Jenny was about to do the same, when she looked down and realized she still had the bag of money in her hands. She gasped, turned on her heel, and bolted back to the bank as fast as her legs would carry her.

But it was too late. The bank had closed. And she had missed her deadline.

Jenny stood there, in front of the door for several long minutes, looking at her reflection in the glass.

She didn't know where she would live now, but as long as she was with Nick, she'd be okay. Because she loved him and love wasn't tied to a place. It resided in the heart. Stewart Davenport could take away her ranch, but she'd keep her past memories and the love of her family safe in her heart forever.

Crossing the street, she stepped through the café's open door. The room was packed. Tales spread faster than wildfire in a small town, and Jenny figured the people couldn't wait to see Nick any more than she could.

Where *was* Nick?

The broad shoulders of two big burly men blocked her view of the back counter, but her heart skipped a beat at the sound of his voice.

"I'm flying back to New York tonight," Nick said to the crowd.

"What about Jenny?" Levi called out. "You still have a few minutes left to win the bet."

Jenny dug her toes into the tips of her boots, listening, but still unable to see.

"No," he said, his voice strained. "I blew it. Jenny will never marry me now."

Never marry him? *No!* Her heart hammered as she squeezed past the two big men and stepped into the open space before them.

"Ten thousand dollars says she will."

Jenny waved a stack of green hundreds in the air and the crowd hushed.

She didn't look at them. Her attention was fixed solely on Nick, whose gaze locked on to hers the moment she spoke.

"You want to marry me?"

"Yes."

Jenny studied his face. The large purple welt on his left cheekbone and the laceration on his upper lip looked horrendous.

But worst of all, Nick's expression remained guarded. She couldn't tell what he was thinking. Did he really care for her or had the light in his eyes, the passion in his kisses all been an act? Her stomach clenched as she waited for a sign.

"Jenny," Nick said, his voice low and even, "I traded Charlie Pickett my three land parcels for his early fire-insurance money. I used it to pay off your bank debt right before the race."

She stared at him, and it took a few moments for his words to sink in.

"You mean the ranch is still mine?"

"Forever and ever."

Jenny gasped. "And you?"

The taut muscles in Nick's face relaxed, his silver-gray eyes sparkled . . . and the wide smile he gave her dispelled every fear that had hovered at the edge of her heart.

Jenny wasn't sure who moved first, but a moment later she was wrapped in a fierce hug, and she was laughing and crying at the same time. Warmth flooded over her and she became light-headed, as if she'd sipped too much of Levi MacGowan's home-brewed whiskey.

"Why?" Nick asked. "Why would you try to trade Windy Meadows for me?"

Jenny pressed her cheek against his chest, the truth never more clear. "I could never love a place as much as I love you."

Nick pulled back with a start. "What did you say?"

"I love you," she repeated, her whole heart behind each word.

Nick grinned. "Will you marry me right now?"

"Yes."

"Don't do it, Jenny!" Charlie shouted. "It's almost one o'clock. If you wait eight more minutes, you'll win the bet."

Jenny shook her head. "I don't want to wait another second."

Nick looked at the man sitting on the bar stool behind him. "Reverend Thornberry, did you hear that?"

The preacher furrowed his brows. "I'm afraid I did."

Nick took her hand and gazed down at her with more passion than she'd ever believed possible.

"I love you, too, Jenny."

Reverend Thornberry began to recite the traditional marriage vow passages. Then he looked at his watch, rolled his eyes heavenward, and threw up his hands.

"May God help you, I now pronounce you husband and wife."

Nick drew her close and kissed her, his lips warm and tender, and full of promises for the future.

"Fifty dollars says their first kid is a boy," Levi called out.

Cheers soared into the air, and empty drink glasses smashed wildly around them, as more and more wagers began to be placed.

Nick smiled against her lips and Jenny couldn't help but laugh. She was more than willing to be part of *this* bet.

Read on for a special early look
at Darlene Panzera's delicious new series

The Cupcake Diaries

Three tempting tales
Three mouthwatering heroes

Coming from Avon Impulse
in May 2013

> "Forget love . . . I'd rather fall in chocolate!"
>
> **Anonymous**

ANDI CAST A GLANCE over the rowdy karaoke crowd to the man sitting at the front table with the clear plastic bakery box in his possession.

"What am I supposed to say?" she whispered, looking back at her dark-haired sister Kim, and their redheaded friend Rachel as the three of them huddled together. " 'Can I have your cupcake?' He'll think I'm a lunatic."

"Say 'please,' and tell him about our tradition," Kim suggested.

"Offer him money." Rachel dug through her dilapidated Gucci knockoff purse and withdrew a ten-dollar bill. "And let him know we're celebrating your sister's birthday."

"You did promise me a cupcake for my birthday," Kim said with an impish grin. "Besides, the guy doesn't look like he plans to eat it. He hasn't even glanced at the cupcake since the old woman came in and delivered the box."

Andi tucked a loose strand of her dark blonde hair behind her ear and drew in a deep breath. She wasn't used to taking food from anyone. Usually she was on the other end—giving it away. Her fault. She didn't plan ahead.

Why couldn't any of the businesses here be open twenty-four hours, like in Portland? Out of the two dozen eclectic cafés and restaurants along the Astoria waterfront promising to satisfy customers' palates, shouldn't at least one cater to late-night customers like herself? No, they all shut down at 10:30 P.M., some earlier, as if they knew she was coming. That's what she got for living in a small town. Anticipation, but no cake.

However, she was determined not to let her younger sister down. She'd promised Kim a cupcake for her twenty-sixth birthday, and she'd try her best to procure one, even if it meant making a fool of herself.

Andi shot her ever-popular friend Rachel a wry look. "You know you're better at this than I am."

Rachel grinned. "You're going to have to start interacting with the opposite sex again sometime."

Maybe. But not on the personal level Rachel's tone suggested. Her divorce the previous year had left behind a bitter aftertaste no amount of sweet talk could dissolve.

Pushing back her chair, Andi stood up. "Tonight, all I want is the cupcake."

Andi had only taken five steps when the man with the bakery box turned his head and smiled.

He probably thought she was coming over, hoping to find a date. Why shouldn't he? The Captain's Port was filled with people looking for a connection. If not for a lifetime, then at least for the few hours they shared within the friendly confines of the restaurant's casual, communal atmosphere.

She hesitated midstep before continuing forward. Heat rushed into her cheeks. Dressed in jeans, and a navy blue tie and sport coat, he was even better-looking than she'd first thought. Thirtyish. Light brown hair, fair skin, sparkling chocolate-brown eyes—*oh, my*. He could have *his* pick of any girl in the place. Any girl in Astoria, Oregon.

"Hi," he said in greeting.

Andi swallowed the nervous tension gathering at the back of her throat and managed a smile in return. "Hi. I'm sorry to bother you, but it's my sister's birthday and I promised her a cupcake." She nodded toward the see-through box and waved the ten-dollar bill. "Is there any chance I can persuade you to sell the one you have here?"

The guy's brows shot up. "You want my cupcake?"

"I meant to bake a batch this afternoon," she gushed, her words stumbling over themselves, "but I ended up packing spring-break lunches for the needy kids in the school district. Have you heard of the Kids Coalition backpack program?"

He nodded. "Yes, I think the *Astoria Sun* featured the

free lunch backpack program on the community page of the newspaper a few weeks ago."

"I'm a volunteer," she explained. "And after I finished, I tried to buy a cupcake but didn't get to the store in time. I've never let my sister down before, and I feel awful."

The handsome man leaned back in his chair and pressed his lips together, as if considering her request, then shook his head. "I'd love to help you, but—"

"*Please*." Andi gasped, appalled she'd stooped to begging. She straightened her shoulders and lifted her chin. "I understand if you can't, it's just that my friend Rachel, my sister Kim, and I have a tradition."

"What kind of tradition?"

Andi pointed to their table, and the other two women smiled and waved. "Our birthdays are all spaced exactly four months apart. So we split a celebration cupcake three ways and set new goals for ourselves from one person's birthday to the next. It's easier than trying to set goals for an entire year."

"I don't suppose you could set your goals without the cupcake?" he asked, his eyes sparkling with amusement.

Andi smiled. "It wouldn't be the same."

"If the cupcake were mine to give, it would be yours. But this particular cupcake was delivered special, for a research project I have at work."

"Wish I had your job." Andi dropped into the chair he pulled out for her and laid her hands flat on the table. "What if I told you it's been a really tough day, tough week, tough year?"

He pushed his empty coffee cup aside and the corners

of his mouth twitched upward. "I'd say I could argue the same."

"But did you spend the last three hours running all over town looking for a cupcake?" she challenged, playfully mimicking Rachel's flirtatious singsong tone. "The Pig 'n' Pancake was closed, along with the supermarket, and the café down the street said they don't even sell them anymore. And then . . . I met you."

He covered her left hand with his own, and although the unexpected contact made her jump, she ignored the impulse to pull her fingers away. His gesture seemed more an act of compassion than anything else and . . . she liked the feel of his firm yet gentle touch.

"What if I told you," he said, leaning forward, "I've traveled five hundred and seventy miles and waited sixty-three days to taste this one cupcake?"

Andi leaned toward him as well. "I'd say that's ridiculous. There's no cupcake in Astoria worth all that trouble."

"What if this particular cupcake isn't from Astoria?"

"No?" She took another look at the box, but couldn't see a label. "Where is it from?"

"Cannon Beach."

"What if I told you I could send you a dozen Cannon Beach cupcakes tomorrow?"

"What if I told *you*," he said, stopping to release a deep throaty chuckle, "this is the last morsel of food I have to eat before I starve to death today?"

Andi laughed. "I'd say that's a good way to go. Or I could invite you to my place and cook you dinner."

Her heart stopped, stunned by her own words, then rebooted a moment later when their gazes locked and he smiled at her.

"You can have the cupcake on one condition."

"Which is?"

Giving her a wink, he slid the clear-sided bakery box toward her. Then he leaned his head in close and whispered in her ear.

About the Author

A graduate of the *Writers' Digest* advanced novel-writing school and the Christian Writers Guild's apprentice program, DARLENE PANZERA is an active member of Romance Writers of America's Greater Seattle and Peninsula Chapters.

Darlene is the winner of the Make Your Dreams Come True contest, sponsored by Avon Books, which led her novella, *The Bet*, to be published within Debbie Macomber's *Family Affair*, released June 2012.

She's also published several short stories, and *A Look of Love* was a top finalist in the *Writer's Digest* Popular Fiction Awards contest.

Born and raised in New Jersey, Darlene now lives in the Pacific Northwest with her husband and three children. When not writing, she enjoys spending time with her family and her two horses, and loves camping, hiking, photography, and lazy days at the lake.

Darlene Panzera would love to hear from her readers. You can find her on Facebook, or write to her at: P.O. Box 1876 Belfair, WA 98528.

Visit her website at www.darlenepanzera.com.

Visit www.AuthorTracker.com for exclusive information on your favorite HarperCollins authors.

Give in to your impulses . . .
Read on for a sneak peek at five brand-new
e-book original tales of romance
from Avon Books.
Available now wherever e-books are sold.

NIGHTS OF STEEL
THE ETHER CHRONICLES
By Nico Rosso

ALICE'S WONDERLAND
By Allison Dobell

ONE FINE FIREMAN
A BACHELOR FIREMEN NOVELLA
By Jennifer Bernard

THERE'S SOMETHING
ABOUT LADY MARY
A Summersby Tale
By Sophie Barnes

THE SECRET LIFE OF LADY LUCINDA
A Summersby Tale
By Sophie Barnes

An Excerpt from

NIGHTS OF STEEL

The Ether Chronicles

by Nico Rosso

Return to The Ether Chronicles, where rival bounty hunters Anna Blue and Jack Hawkins join forces to find a mysterious fugitive, only to get so much more than they bargained for. The skies above the American West are about to get wilder than ever . . .

Take his hand? Or walk down the broken stairs to chase a cold trail. Anna's body was still buffeted by waves of sensation. The meal was an adventure she shared with Jack. Nearly falling from the stairs, only to be brought close to his body, had been a rush. The hissing of the lodge was the last bit of danger, but it had passed.

The wet heat of that simple room was inviting. Her joints

and bones ached for comfort. Deeper down, she yearned for Jack. They'd been circling each other for years. The closer she got—hearing his voice, touching his skin, learning his history—the more the hunger increased. She didn't know where it would lead her, but she had to find out. All she had to do was take his hand.

Anna slid her palm against his. Curled her fingers around him. He held her hand, staring into her eyes. She'd thought she knew the man behind the legend and the metal and the guns, yet now she understood there were miles of territory within him she had yet to discover.

Their grips tightened. They drew closer. He leaned down to her. She pressed against his chest. In the sunlight, they kissed. Neither hid their hunger. She understood his need. His lips on hers were strong, devouring. And she understood her yearning. Probing forward with her tongue, she led him into her.

And it wasn't enough. Their first kiss could've taken them too far and she'd had to stop. Now, with Jack pressed against her, his arm wrapped around her shoulders and his lips against hers, too far seemed like the perfect place to go.

They pulled apart and, each still gripping the other's hand, walked back into the lodge room. Sheets of steam curled up the walls and filled the space, bringing out the scent of the redwood paneling. The room seemed alive, breathing with her.

Jack cracked a small smile. "This guy, Song, I like his style. Lot of inventors are drunk on tetrol. Half-baked ideas that don't work right." He held up his half-mechanical hand. "People wind up getting hurt."

"Song knows his business," she agreed. "So why the bounty?"

He leveled his gaze at her. It seemed the steam came from him, his intensity. "You want a cold trail or a hot bath?"

She took off her hat, holding his look and not backing down. "Hot. Bath."

Burbling invitingly like a secluded brook, the tub waited in the corner. The steam softened its edges and obscured the walls around it. As if the room went on forever.

With the toe of his boot, Jack swung the front door closed. Only the small lights in the ceiling glowed. Warm night clouds now surrounded her. A gentle storm. And Jack was the lightning. Still gripping her hand, he walked her toward the tub, chuckling a little to himself.

"My last bath was at a lonely little stage stop hotel in Camarillo."

The buckle on her gun belt was hot from the steam. "I'm overdue." She undid it and held the rig in her hand.

"I'm guessing you picked up Malone's trail sometime after the Sierras, so it's been a few hundred miles for you, too."

It took her a second to track her path backward. "Beatty, Nevada."

"Rough town." He let go of her hand so he could undo the straps and belts that held his own weapons.

She hung her gun belt on a wooden peg on the wall next to the tub. Easy to reach if she had to. "A little less rough after I left."

His pistols and quad shotgun took their place next to her weapons. He was unarmed. But still deadly. Broad shoulders, muscled arms and legs. Dark, blazing eyes. And the smallest smile.

They came together again, this time without the clang of gunmetal. The heat of the room had soaked through her clothes, bringing a light sweat across her skin. She felt every fold of fabric, and every ridge of his muscles. Her hands ran over the cords of his neck, pulling him to her mouth for another kiss.

Nerves yearned for sensation. Dust storms had chafed her flesh. Ice-cold rivers had woken her up, and she'd slept in the rain while waiting out a fugitive. She needed pleasure. And Jack was the only man strong enough to bring it to her.

An Excerpt from

ALICE'S WONDERLAND
by Allison Dobell

**When journalist and notorious womanizer
Flynn O'Grady publicly mocks Alice Mitchell's
erotic luxury goods website, the game is on. They
soon find themselves locked in a sensual battle
where Alice must step up the spice night after
night as, one by one, Flynn's defenses crumble.**

AN AVON RED NOVELLA

Flynn O'Grady had gone too far this time. It was bad enough
that Sydney Daily's resident male blogger continued to push
his low opinions about women into the community (he
seemed to have an ongoing problem with shoes and shopping), but this time he'd mentioned her business by name.

How dare he suggest she was a charlatan, promising the

world and delivering nothing! The women who came to Alice's Wonderland were discerning, educated, and thoroughly in charge of their sexuality. They loved to play and knew the value in paying for quality. They knew the difference between her beautiful artisan-made, hand-carved, silver-handled spanking paddle (of which she'd moved over 500 units this past financial year, she might add) and a $79.95 mass-produced Taiwanese purple plastic dildo from hihosilver.com.

Still, while Alice didn't agree with the raunch culture that prevailed at hihosilver, she'd defend (with one of their cheap dildos raised high) the right of any woman to take on a Tickler, Rabbit, or Climax Gem in the privacy of her own home. Where was it written that men had cornered the market for liking sex? O'Grady had clearly been under a rock for at least three decades.

Alice reached for the old-fashioned cream-and-gold telephone on her glass-topped desk and dialed. She knew what she needed to do to make a man like Flynn O'Grady understand where she was coming from. As the phone rang, she re-read the blog entry for the third time. Anger rose within her, but she pushed it down. She'd need her wits about her for this conversation.

"O'Grady."

Alice took a deep breath before she began. "Mr. O'Grady, we haven't met, but you seem to know all about me."

A brief silence on the other end.

"I see," came the answer. "Would you care to elaborate?" His voice was deep and husky around the edges. He should have been in radio, rather than in print.

"Alice Mitchell here. Purveyor of broken promises."

Another pause.

"Ms. Mitchell, how . . . delightful." His tone made it clear that it was anything but.

"I'm sure," said Alice, raising one eyebrow slightly, allowing her smile to warm her words. "You've had quite a lot to say about my business today. I was wondering if we could meet. I think I deserve the right of reply."

"I'm not sure what good that would do, Ms. Mitchell," he replied, smoothly. "You're more than welcome to respond via the comments section on my blog."

She'd had the feeling he'd try that.

"I think this is more . . . personal than that," Alice purred down the line. "I'd like to try to convince you of my . . . position." She stifled a laugh, enjoying every second of this. She could easily imagine him squirming in his chair right now.

The silence that followed inched toward uncomfortable.

"Er, right. Well, I don't have any time today, but I could see you on Wednesday," he said.

It was Monday. Give him all day Tuesday to plan his defenses? Not likely.

"It would be great if you could make it today," she said, a hint of steel entering her tone. "I'd hate to have to take this to your boss. I suspect there may be grounds for a defamation complaint, but I'm sure the two of us can work it out . . ." She left the idea dangling. The media was no place for job insecurity in the current climate, and she knew he was too smart not to know that. He needed to keep his boss happy.

"I could fit you in tonight, but it would need to be after 7.30," he said, his voice carefully controlled.

'"Perfect," she said, "I'll come to your office."

She put down the phone, allowing him no time to answer, then sat back in her chair. Now all she needed to do was select an item or two that would help her to convince Flynn he should change his mind.

Standing quickly, she prowled over to the open glass shelving that took up one wall of her domain. Although it might be of use in getting her point across, it was probably too soon for the geisha gag. She didn't know him well enough to bring out the tooled leather slave-style handcuffs. Wait a minute! She almost spanked herself with the paddle that Flynn O'Grady had derided for overlooking the obvious.

Moving to a small glass cabinet in the corner, she opened the top drawer and inspected the silken blindfolds. She picked up a scarlet one and held it, delicate and cool to the touch, in her hand.

Perfect.

An Excerpt from

ONE FINE FIREMAN

A Bachelor Firemen Novella

by Jennifer Bernard

**What happens when you mix together an
absolutely gorgeous fireman, a beautiful but
shy woman, her precocious kid, and a very
mischievous little dog? Find out in Jennifer
Bernard's sizzling hot *One Fine Fireman*.**

The door opened, and three firemen walked in. Maribel
nearly dropped the Lazy Morning Specials in table six's lap.
Goodness, they were like hand grenades of testosterone rolling in the door, sucking all the air out of the room. They wore
dark blue t-shirts tucked into their yellow firemen's pants, thick
suspenders holding up the trousers. They walked with rolling
strides, probably because of their big boots. Individually they
were handsome, but collectively they were devastating.

Maribel knew most of the San Gabriel firemen by name. The brown-haired one with eyes the color of a summer day was Ryan Blake. The big, bulky guy with the intimidating muscles was called Vader. She had no idea what his real name was, but apparently the nickname came from the way he loved to make spooky voices with his breathing apparatus. The third one trailed behind the others, and she couldn't make out his identity. Then Ryan took a step forward, revealing the man behind him. She sucked in a breath.

Kirk was back. For months she'd been wondering where he was and been too shy to ask. She'd worried that he'd transferred to another town, or decided to chuck it all and sail around the world. She'd been half afraid she'd never see him again. But here he was, in the flesh, just as mouthwatering as ever. Her face heated as she darted glance after glance at him, like a starving person just presented with prime rib. It was wrong, so wrong; she was engaged. But she couldn't help it. She had to see if everything about him was as she remembered.

His silvery gray-green eyes, the exact color of the sagebrush that grew in the hills around San Gabriel, hadn't changed, though he looked more tired than she remembered. His blond hair, which he'd cut drastically since she'd last seen him, picked up glints of sunshine through the plate glass window. His face looked thinner, maybe older, a little pale. But his mouth still had that secret humorous quirk. The rest of his face usually held a serious expression, but his mouth told a different story. It was as if he hid behind a quiet mask, but his mouth had chosen to rebel. Not especially tall, he had a powerful, quiet presence and a spectacular physique under his firefighter gear. She noticed that, unlike the others, he wore a long-sleeved shirt.

His fellow firefighters called him Thor. She could certainly see why. He looked like her idea of a Viking god, though she would imagine the God of Thunder would be more of a loudmouth. Kirk was not a big talker. He didn't say much, but when he spoke, people seemed to listen.

She certainly did, even though all he'd said to her was, "Black, no sugar," and "How much are those little Christmas ornaments?" referring to the beaded angels she made for sale during the holidays. It was embarrassing how much she relived those little moments afterward.

Tossing friendly smiles to the other customers, the three men strolled to the counter where she took the orders. They gathered around the menu board, though why they bothered, she didn't know. They always ordered the same thing. Firemen seemed to be creatures of habit. Or at least her firemen were.

An Excerpt from

THERE'S SOMETHING ABOUT LADY MARY

A SUMMERSBY TALE

by Sophie Barnes

When Mary Croyden inherits a title and a
large sum of money, she must rely on the help
of one man—Ryan Summersby. But Mary's
hobbies are not exactly proper, and Ryan is
starting to realize that this simple miss is
not at all what he expected . . . in the second
Summersby Tale from Sophie Barnes.

Mary stepped back. Had she really forgotten to introduce
herself? Was it possible that Ryan Summersby didn't know
who she really was? She suddenly dreaded having to tell him.
She'd enjoyed spending time with him, had even considered
the possibility of seeing him again, but once he knew her true

identity, he'd probably treat her no differently than all the other gentlemen had done—like a grand pile of treasure with which to pay off his debts and house his mistresses.

Squaring her shoulders and straightening her spine, she mustered all her courage and turned a serious gaze upon him. "My name is Mary Croyden, and I am the Marchioness of Steepleton."

Ryan's response was instantaneous. His mouth dropped open while his eyes widened in complete and utter disbelief. He stared at the slender woman who stood before him, doing her best to play the part of a peeress. Was it really possible that she was the very marchioness he'd been looking for when he'd stepped outside for some fresh air only half an hour earlier? The very same one that Percy had asked him to protect? She seemed much too young for such a title, too unpolished. It wasn't that he found her unattractive in any way, though he had thought her plain at first glance.

"What?" she asked, as she crossed her arms and cocked an eyebrow. "Not what you expected the infamous Marchioness of Steepleton to look like?"

"Not exactly, no," he admitted. "You are just not—"

"Not what? Not pretty enough? Not sophisticated enough? Or is it perhaps that the way in which I speak fails to equate with your ill-conceived notion of what a marchioness ought to sound like?" He had no chance to reply before she said, "Well, you do not exactly strike me as a stereotypical medical student either."

"And just what exactly would you know about that?" he asked, a little put out by her sudden verbal attack.

"Enough," she remarked in a rather clipped tone. "My

father was a skilled physician. I know the sort of man it takes to fill such a position, and you, my lord, do not fit the bill."

For the first time in his life, Ryan Summersby found himself at a complete loss for words. Not only could he not comprehend that this slip of a woman before him, appearing to be barely out of the schoolroom, was a peeress in her own right—not to mention a woman of extreme wealth. But that she was actually standing there, fearlessly scolding him . . . he knew that a sane person would be quite offended, and yet he couldn't help but be enthralled.

In addition, he'd also managed to glimpse a side of her that he very much doubted many people had ever seen. "You do not think too highly of yourself, do you?" He suddenly asked.

That brought her up short. "I have no idea what you could possibly mean by that," she told him defensively.

"Well, you assume that I do not believe you to be who you say you are. You think the reasoning behind my not believing you might have something to do with the way you look. Finally, you feel the need to assert yourself by finding fault with me—for which I must commend you, since I do not have very many faults at all."

"You arrogant . . ." The marchioness wisely clamped her mouth shut before uttering something that she would be bound to regret. Instead, she turned away and walked toward the French doors that led toward the ballroom. "Thank you for the dance, Mr. Summersby. I hope you enjoy the rest of your evening," she called over her shoulder in an obvious attempt at sounding dignified.

"May I call on you sometime?" he asked, ignoring her

abrupt dismissal of him as he thought of the task that Percy had given him. It really wouldn't do for him to muck things up so early in the game. And besides, he wasn't sure he'd ever met a woman who interested him more than Lady Steepleton did at that very moment. He had to admit that the woman had character.

She paused in the middle of her exit, turned slightly, and looked him dead in the eye. "You most certainly may not, Mr. Summersby." And before Ryan had a chance to dispute the matter, she had vanished back inside, the white cotton of her gown twirling about her feet.

An Excerpt from

THE SECRET LIFE OF LADY LUCINDA

A SUMMERSBY TALE

by Sophie Barnes

Lucy Blackwell throws caution to the wind when she tricks Lord William Summersby into a marriage of convenience. But she never counted on falling in love . . .

"Do you love her?" Miss Blackwell suddenly asked, her head tilted upward at a slight angle.

Lord, even her voice was delightful to listen to. And those imploring eyes of hers . . . No, he'd be damned if he'd allow her to ensnare him with her womanly charms. She'd practically made fools of both his sister and his father—she'd get no sympathy from him. Not now, not ever. "You and I are hardly well enough acquainted with one another for you to take such liberties in your questions, Miss Blackwell. My relationship to Lady Annabelle is of a personal nature, and certainly not one that I am about to discuss with you."

Miss Blackwell blinked. "Then you do not love her," she said simply.

"I hold her in the highest regard," he said.

Miss Blackwell stared back at him with an increased measure of doubt in her eyes. "More reason for me to believe that you do not love her."

"Miss Blackwell, if I did not know any better, I should say that you are either mad or deaf—perhaps even both. At no point have I told you that I do not love her, yet you are quite insistent upon the matter."

"That is because, my lord, it is in everything you are saying and everything that you are not. If you truly loved her, you would not have had a moment's hesitation in professing it. It is therefore my belief that you do not love her but are marrying her simply out of obligation."

Why the blazes he was having this harebrained conversation with a woman he barely even knew, much less liked, was beyond him. But the beginnings of a smile that now played upon her lips did nothing short of make him catch his breath. With a sigh of resignation, he slowly nodded his head. "Well done, Miss Blackwell. You have indeed found me out."

Her smile broadened. "Then it really doesn't matter whom you marry, as long as you marry. Is that not so?"

He frowned, immediately on guard at her sudden enthusiasm. "Not exactly, no. The woman I marry must be one of breeding, of a gentle nature and graceful bearing. Lady Annabelle fits all of those criteria rather nicely, and, in time, I am more than confident that we shall become quite fond of one another."

The impossible woman had the audacity to roll her eyes. "All I really wanted to know was whether or not anyone's heart might be jeopardized if you were persuaded to marry somebody else. That is all."

"Miss Blackwell, I can assure you that I have no intention of marrying anyone other than Lady Annabelle. She and I have a mutual agreement. We are both honorable people. Neither one of us would ever consider going back on his word."

"I didn't think as much," she mused, and before William had any time to consider what she might be about to do, she'd thrown her arms around his neck, pulled him toward her, and placed her lips against his.